GUNFIGHT AT LARAMIE

GUNFIGHT AT LARAMIE

LEE HOFFMAN

THORNDIKE
CHIVERS

This Large Print edition is published by Thorndike Press, Waterville, Maine, USA and by AudioGO Ltd, Bath, England.

Thorndike Press, a part of Gale, Cengage Learning.

LIBRARY OF CONGRESS CATALOGING-IN-PUBLICATION DATA

Hoffman, Lee, 1932–
    Gunfight at Laramie / by Lee Hoffman.
      p. cm. — (Thorndike Press large print Western)
    ISBN-13: 978-1-4104-3230-8 (hardcover)
    ISBN-10: 1-4104-3230-0 (hardcover)
    1. Large type books. I. Title.
  PS3558.O346G86 2010
  813'.54—dc22   2010037046

BRITISH LIBRARY CATALOGUING-IN-PUBLICATION DATA AVAILABLE

Published in 2010 in the U.S. by arrangement with Golden West Literary Agency.

Published in 2011 in the U.K. by arrangement with Golden West Literary Agency.

U.K. Hardcover: 978 1 408 49381 6 (Chivers Large Print)
U.K. Softcover: 978 1 408 49382 3 (Camden Large Print)

Printed in the United States of America
1 2 3 4 5 6 7 14 13 12 11 10

GUNFIGHT AT LARAMIE

I

"Ain't she a queen?" the engineer said. He smiled broadly at his passenger as he turned away from the steam gauge. "She's the pride of the Baldwin works and the U.P. line."

The stoker paused and glanced up, grinning. His face was shining with sweat and against his smoke-darkened skin his eyes glistened from the flow of the open firebox. "Mike thinks more of this big hog than he does of his wife and kids," he said.

"How many kids you got now?" the cab passenger asked.

"Five," Mike answered. "Mebbe six by the time I get back to Omaha." He cocked his head, listening to the steady rhythm of the drivers pounding on the rails, the rattle of the pony truck and the snorting hiss of exhausting steam. Fast enough for night-running, he thought. But the big diamond-stacked Mogul had full pressure and a clear track straight through to the railroad con-

7

struction camp.

Satisfied, he leaned a shoulder against the window frame and looked at the cab passenger. "It's sure good to see you again, Dev. When things went wrong down in Georgia we figured you was dead. Then word come through that the Rebs had caught you, but from what I heard about them Secsech prison camps. . . ."

The man called Dev looked into the engineer's face, trying to read his eyes in the flickering light from the firebox. "I got exchanged with some of the other wounded," he said. "You heard about me since the war, didn't you, Mike?"

The engineer shrugged. "I heard something about you working for the D.S. & F.M. back in Illinois."

"Yeah," Dev muttered. He turned to gaze out the window at the weird patterns of silver and black that the moonlight slashed out of the rising peaks ahead. The chill wind whipped at the long fringes on the sleeves of his buckskin shirt.

"I heard about it," Mike said. There was a finality in his voice as if he were willing to let the subject be dropped.

For a long moment there was no sound but the thunder of the locomotive. Then the engineer spoke in a casual way: "From the look of your clothes you ain't railroading no more."

Dev glanced down at the greasy buckskin shirt, the cord breeches tucked into the tops of his boots and the tarnished chains of his spurs. "No," he said. Then almost apologetically he added, "I've been skinning for a crew of buffalo hunters."

"Is that what's bringing you out here to Hell-on-Wheels?"

"Not exactly. I'm looking for a man I heard might be out here. Fellow name of Danforth."

Mike shook his head slowly. " 'Fraid I don't know many of the gang at End-of-Track. Somebody you knew in the war?"

"Somebody I knew in Illinois." There was an edge of bitterness in Dev's voice. He turned back to the window. The wind caught at his dark hair, flailing it against his face. When he leaned out he could see the white *extra* flag on the pilot, flashing in the spill from the whale-oil lamp mounted over the smoke box. Ahead the rails were shining in the beam of the headlamp. And even beyond the throw of the lamp they gleamed dully in the moonlight, twin bands of steel running toward each other until — oh, God!

Jerking his head around, Dev shouted, "Brakes!"

The engineer's hand was reaching for the whistle cord as he thrust his head out of the cab. He yanked the cord and the whistle screamed for the brakemen.

Leaning through the window, Dev could see it clearly now. The thin silver line of the track was broken. A section of rail had been lifted.

The engine groaned and squealed as the flow of steam to its cylinders was reversed, the pressure now fighting against the pounding pistons, straining against the momentum of the huge locomotive. Iron screamed on iron as the brakemen atop the cars thrust their clubs into the spokes of the hand-wheels, dogging them around, bringing the brake shoes to bear against the truck wheels. But they were going too fast — the gap was too close — the heavy supply train couldn't be hauled down in time.

"Jump!"

Dev heard the engineer's shout. He looked around in time to see the fireman throw himself from the cab. The man was tense, thrashing his arms as he jumped. Then Mike wheeled and Dev saw the engineer's big hands outthrust.

"Jump!" Mike shouted again as he shoved against Dev's chest.

Dev felt the hands, felt himself stumbling

backward. He threw back a foot to brace himself. He stepped into nothingness. He fell.

He was tumbling over the rough rock of the roadbed ballast. The speeding train loomed almost overhead. The freight cars bobbed on their trucks as the wheels hammered past him, spitting yellow sparks against the brake shoes. He glimpsed a figure — a man jumping from atop one of the cars. He saw the mass of stars overhead spinning wildly. The sights were fragmentary, piled one on top of another, careening as he fell.

And then he was lying still, sprawled on his face in the dew-damp buffalo grass. Raising his head, he saw the caboose roll by. Suddenly the rhythm of the pounding wheels broke. The train lurched, veering as it lunged forward. For an instant there was a piercing, scraping sound that jarred across his nerves.

He saw the engine lean, then totter and topple, dragging cars over with it. As it rolled onto its side the world was filled with thunder. A sudden, brilliant white light filled his vision, burning into his eyes. For a moment he was blinded by it.

The boiler had burst.

He pressed a hand against his face. A

breath of warm air touched him and then was gone. When he drew his hand away he saw the fire. Raging flames were enveloping the shambles of twisted metal that had been the pride of the Baldwin locomotive works.

The wind whipped at the flames and fire spilled out. It bit into the prairie grass and raced along, crawling up the walls of the splintered boxcars and the shattered caboose. In minutes, it would be eating into those cars, through the bales of raw cotton that had been used for packing, and into the kegs of blasting powder.

Dev dragged himself to his feet. His body was without feeling, his mind detached, and it took effort to make his muscles respond. He ran.

There was a depression of some kind in the field just ahead of him. He could see the dark shadow of it winding across the fire-lit plain. He stumbled toward it and threw himself down into the shadow.

It was a creek. He found himself on his belly in about a foot of water. He lay there — waiting — holding his breath while the chill stream flowed over him.

The blast came. The water muffled the sound and he heard it as if from a far distance. It was a series of blasts, one on top of another, like bombs exploding during an artillery shelling. The sound of the bursting locomotive boiler had been different somehow. And somehow more terrible.

His lungs were beginning to ache and his chest muscles tried to jerk air into them. He raised his head above the water, gasping to catch his breath. Craning his neck, he looked back over his shoulder at the flaming wreckage. Had Mike been able to escape, he wondered. He doubted it.

Shaking his head, he sat up. He felt sick. Godawful sick. As he looked up at it, the moon seemed to quaver and twist, dividing itself into two discs that danced around each other. And then suddenly it was snuffed out. The world became a thick blackness that washed over him and he felt himself falling through bottomless dark.

The pain in his head was a sharp, throbbing kind, like a piston hammering inside his skull. As from a distance, he could hear the sounds of an idling locomotive and the excited, shouting voices of men. Slowly, he realized that the sounds were nearby. He forced his eyes open and looked up, into a face. Squinting, he brought it into focus. It was a familiar face. A hand near it was holding a lantern that washed its features in warm yellow light. The brows were drawn together into a creased, questioning frown and the lips puckered slightly.

Looking into the face, Dev muttered, "Evenin', Major."

The hand that held the lantern moved and shadows played across the face. He couldn't be sure whether it was scowling or grinning. "Damnit, Devereaux," the man said. "How the hell did *you* get into this?"

"You ain't in uniform, Major," Dev heard himself saying. "Are you pounding brass now?"

"Hell no, I'm supercargo. Representative of a bunch of investors in the Union Pacific. What happened here? Jump a joint?"

He propped himself up on one elbow and rubbed at the back of his neck. "It wasn't any accident. Somebody pulled out a rail."

"Goddamnit," the major grunted. "This time they've done it good. First spikes, now rails."

Dev looked toward the track, at the engine idling there and the single flatcar coupled behind it. There were men on the flatcar, more men scurrying back and forth between the emergency train and the wreck, fighting the remains of the fire, prodding at the rubble with shovels and some just milling, looking. He asked, "Did anyone else get out?"

The major's dark eyes searched his face. "Three. And you. You *were* on that train, weren't you?"

Dev nodded. The motion aggravated the ache in his head. He pressed a hand to his temple. He could feel the throbbing of the pulse there through his fingertips.

"Why?" the major was asking.

Dev looked at him blankly.

"What were you doing on that train?"

Was there any reason to lie, he asked himself. "I hitched a ride from Hazard. Mike Connor was hogging it, you know."

"I know. I remember Mike. You and he were pretty good friends back when you were in the U.S.M.R., weren't you? Have you kept in touch with each other since the war?"

"No, sir. This was the first time I've seen him since I got into that mission in Georgia." Dev turned his head and looked at the twisted remains of the Mogul. He asked, "Dead?"

"We haven't found him yet. Maybe we never will."

"He told me he was expecting another kid. The sixth."

The major nodded as he gazed at the wreckage. Then he turned back to Dev.

15

"What were you doing hitching a ride out here?"

"Just drifting. Looking for a job."

"You were booming on the U.P.? You know the Union Pacific wouldn't hire *you*, Devereaux."

"I know." Dev muttered. Hesitantly, he asked, "You heard about it?"

"I saw the newspaper accounts and I heard the reports of the investigating committee," the major mumbled. "Hell of a mess."

Dev nodded. He could tell from the man's silence that he was waiting for an explanation of some kind, but he offered none.

Still frowning, the major asked, "Can you prove you were on this train? Did anyone at Hazard see you there?"

"I don't think so. I was kinda keeping myself out of sight."

"Why?"

"I figured on hopping the blinds until I saw it was Mike in the cab. Then I waved him and asked him for a ride." Dev rubbed at his forehead. His head still ached and his thoughts weren't at all clear. Why all the questions, he wondered. They didn't seem to make sense. He said, "Maybe one of the brakemen saw me. Why?"

"You could be in trouble. Bad trouble. To

be mixed up in a thing like this — twice. There'll be an investigation."

It took a moment for understanding to seep into his mind. Startled, he looked into the dark eyes and asked, "You don't think I had a hand in wrecking Mike, do you, Major Nordstadt?"

The major fingered his moustache. Finally, he said, "No, *I* don't. But God help you if you can't prove to the Union Pacific that you were *on* that train and not here at trackside. . . ."

II

Dev woke slowly. He became aware that he was lying on a cot, under a sunlit roof of canvas. For an instant, he thought he was back in the army hospital tent. But then he remembered.

From the look of it, this was one of the workers' tents at End-of-Track. And he had just wakened from a nightmare that was no dream. The vision of the toppling locomotive and the roar of the exploding boiler were still strong in his mind.

He ran a hand over his face, rubbing at his eyes. Then he looked at the shirt he wore. It was faded gray flannel. It wasn't his. Neither were the pants he was wearing.

Whose, he wondered. Not Major Nord-stadt's. And what had become of his own buckskin shirt and cord breeches? And the rest of his gear — the warbag with his clothes and the money he'd saved? And the Sharps & Hankins carbine he'd carried across the plain? Then he remembered the warbag and gun had been left in the loco-motive. They were probably white ash now.

He got up and walked to the mirror that hung from one of the tent poles. Pushing the lank, black hair back off his forehead, he looked at the dark eyes of the image in the mirror. They were red-rimmed and weary and his jaws were flecked with bristles too sparse to ever grow into a decent beard. The face was lean, sharp-boned, naturally dark and heavily tanned. He ran a hand over it, wondering where he could borrow a razor. Maybe from Major Nordstadt.

He thought back over the wreck. Only three others had lived. The two brakemen who'd jumped had come through without serious injury, but neither of them could recall a cab passenger. Only Jake Webb could do that. And Jake, the stoker, had been found at trackside unconscious — close to death.

He remembered talking to the major, walking around the rubble and then riding back to the railhead camp on the flatcar, hunkering protectively beside the blanket-wrapped form of Jake Webb like a watchdog. Jake *might* live, the doctor had said. Or he might stop breathing without ever waking.

Dev gazed into the mirror, thinking that he had to see the major and find out what else had happened the night before. He had to find out what his own position at the present might be. If Jake died . . .

He lifted the tent flap and stepped out into the mid-morning sun. Shading his eyes, he looked around the camp. It set him in mind of the army camps he'd seen back when he enlisted. Or maybe a mess of them, all jumbled together. It was vast and crowded, with a bustling haphazard quality about the array of tents and makeshift shelters that were crammed together in the basin.

Someone shouted, "Hey, you!"

It was a woman's voice and he wheeled to look for her.

"Yes, you, y'black Firbolg!" she called at him. Resting her knuckles on her hips, she looked at him with golden eyes from a face covered with freckles and framed with fire-bright copper hair. Behind her, long strings of laundry fanned out in the breeze. She was scowling fiercely, but there was laughter in the golden eyes. "You come back here with the Fitzpatrick's britches!"

He started toward her. "I'm afraid . . ."

She interrupted, "Afraid, is it? Well, like as not your own britches will be drying about now. But that hide shirt, it's the Dear's own invention. I near took my knuckles down to the bone scrubbing it with glycerine soap inside and out and it's still as greasy as a tallowpot's rag. What have you been soaking it in, buffalo fat?"

"Yes," he said, grinning. "You've been washing my clothes?"

"I couldn't stand the smell of 'em in the camp," she snapped at him. "You're worse than a grader. You'd a smell like a hide skinner when you came into camp last night."

"I *am* a hide skinner."

Behind the freckles, her face turned a glowing red. "Of all the low, lying . . . the major said you was a friend of his and I gave you the lend of the Fitzpatrick's old britches, thinking you was a railroad man."

Her words had reminded him and he asked, "You know where I might find the major now?"

"He'd be in his traveling car, I suppose."

"On the track over there?"

"And where else would his traveling car be?"

20

"I'm obliged," Dev said with a nod.

As he turned toward the rails, she called after him: "You'll be bringing back the Fitzpatrick's britches or he'll show you a few things about skinning, you black Firbolg!"

He grinned. He was still grinning when he reached the track.

The major's car was a weathered old caboose with a stile up to the side door. He stepped up and knocked. From inside came a bellowed, "Ease your fist and come on in."

As Dev pushed open the door the warm smell of frying bacon hit him in the face. Inside the car, Major Nordstadt and a tall, graying Negro, were seated at the folded-down table. It was spread with food.

"Morning, Devereaux," the major said heartily. "Ate yet?"

"No, sir."

"Fetch yourself a plate and join in." He gestured toward a small cupboard with his fork. "And that 'sir' isn't required here."

"Habit, I reckon," Dev mumbled as he reached down a plate. He seated himself at the table.

The major nodded toward his companion, "Noah, this is Corporal Devereaux, formerly of the United States Military Railway system. Dev, Noah Freedman, my secretary and good right hand. He's an old railroader

21

himself. Was with the underground railway in Tennessee for ten years."

Dev mumbled a greeting at the Negro but his attention was on Major Nordstadt. "How's Jake Webb?"

"Still unconscious, but I've left word for them to call me as soon as anything happens. Last I heard, he was resting easy."

"Until he wakens, what about me?"

"I had a talk with General Jack — Jack Casement. Told him the same thing you told me about your booming and hitching a ride with Mike. Told him you'd served in my office during the war. That's all. But he wants to have a talk with you."

"Is he likely to know about me?"

"I doubt if he'll recognize the name. Most people don't pay much heed to the names in newspapers unless they're personally concerned or know the people involved. And he's got no reason to check the blacklist for you."

At the major's words, Dev shot a concerned glance toward Noah Freedman.

"You don't have to worry about Noah," the Major said. "You won't meet a more discreet man. He knows every secret I've got and more besides. I'll trust Noah at any price."

Dev took a good look at the Negro. He

was about the same age as the major, and wore a black broadcloth suit of the same common cut. From his face and his bearing, he looked to be a man who'd pride himself on his good name and the value of his word.

"Well, what about it, Corporal?" the Major said.

"What about what, sir?"

"You're not wandering around the U. P. just to watch the cars roll by. You've come here for some reason. I'd like to know what it is. If you're going to cause trouble, I'd like a chance to be prepared for it."

Hesitantly, Dev told him, "I'm looking for somebody. A bast— a telegraph operator name of Charlie Danforth."

"Danforth? You mean that curly-headed romeo that always smelled of lavender?"

"He *is* here?"

"He *was* here. He quit the U. P. and moved up ahead to Laramie. I don't know what kind of vein he hit. He's not working, but he's living off the top of the hog. I suppose he found some hardworking woman to support him at last. From what I hear he's been hanging around a fancy saloon called the Palace and spending money like he owned the place. There's wire to Laramie if you want to call ahead and inquire."

"No. If Danforth got word I'm this close he'd probably haul his freight."

The major raised an eyebrow. "Then I take it he's not a friend of yours?"

"Not hardly," Dev answered. "He's the one who testified against me at the investigation."

"Oh. And you're here to even the score with him?"

"I intend to get the truth out of him."

The major leaned back in his chair and gazed at Devereaux. "I've read about it in the papers and the committee report. Suppose you tell me your version of what happened. And start at the beginning. How was Danforth involved?"

"He was night operator at Willis Siding. He'd drifted in and gotten the job a couple of months before, and I figured he was the kind who'd be drifting on in another couple. But he had a good fist and he was an agreeable sort. He never objected to standing part of my shift when I — when I needed him to."

"You mean when you were drunk?"

"Yes, damnit, when I was drunk!"

"I recall you got into scrapes when you were in my outfit, but mostly fistfights and that kind of thing. I don't remember you were given much to heavy drinking." It was a question.

"After I got out of that army hospital I still had trouble with my leg," Dev answered. "It would get to paining me, but whiskey helped. So when it got really bad I'd wake up Charlie and he'd spell me at the key. That was when I'd get drunk. It was the only time. I swear it!"

"Easy, I'm not accusing — only asking. But it seems to me there were witnesses that Danforth was in town when that train was wrecked."

"Yeah. But he lied about my drinking. He told that investigating committee that I was drunk most of the time. He said he used to find me sleeping it off at the key and that was a damned lie! When the Special went off the track I wasn't drunk or asleep, either one!"

"Brakes," the major said, gesturing for Dev to calm down. "Slow and easy, just tell me what happened."

Dev nodded and took a breath. He began slowly. "Well, J. B. Hendon was on his way to Chicago for some sort of special board of directors' meeting and the Special was hauling his private car. He had a clear track and I had my orders to send him through fast. I'd set my switch and run up the highball and headed back into the shack and that was the last thing I knew for a while. Somebody must have been waiting for me and slugged me when I walked inside." He rubbed at the back of his head as if he could still feel the pain of the blow.

"I woke up lying across the key with my shirt soaked with whiskey," he continued. "There were some local farmers bending over me and they swore later that they found me stone drunk. I couldn't blame them for that, though. I was pretty groggy and the whole place stank of likker."

"Exactly what happened to the Special?" the major asked.

"When it came through, the switch was only half closed. The train hit it hard and jumped. It piled up and a fire started in Hendon's car. The whole thing was flames by the time those farmers got there. Hendon was the only one who got out alive and they said it was a miracle he did. The car burnt completely. But when the wrecking crew had finished and the Pinkertons had gone over the ground, it came out he'd had close to ten thousand dollars in a safebox in the car and there wasn't a sign of it left. It wouldn't have burnt to ash, but they couldn't find a trace of it."

"Stolen?"

Dev nodded. "They speculated that some

of the wrecking crew might have got it, but most of the talk was that the wreck hadn't been an accident. They tried to make out that I'd set it up so the train could be robbed. There was no evidence, though. Nothing to prove I'd done worse than get drunk and foul the switch. But even after the investigation and the hearing, they had Pinks on my trail. They may still have, but I think I lost 'em on the buffalo range."

"You believe Danforth was the man behind it?"

"Major, the way I figure, there had to be at least two of them. Danforth set me up and half-cocked the switch. Then he high-tailed it to town so he could be seen there. Someone else was on the train, to get hold of the money and get off before the engine hit that switch. Hendon swore that nobody could have gotten into his car before the wreck without him knowing it, but I've ridden the boxes and hid from the brakies often enough and I don't think getting into a private car would be so much different. Only Hendon being the president of the railroad, his word carried weight. Mine didn't."

The major fished into the pocket of his coat. He brought out a pipe and busied himself filling it. Then he asked, "Do you have any evidence to back up your idea?"

"Nothing but what I know to be true — I wasn't drunk and Danforth lied about my drinking to the committee. I couldn't prove it. I could hardly get them to listen to me. They didn't give a damn who they hanged as long as they pinned the blame somewhere. It was my station and my shift, so it was my responsibility. I was just damned lucky they didn't decide to make some kind of criminal charge against me and . . ." He started at the sudden knock at the door.

Scowling, the major put down his pipe and called, "Who is it?"

"Keasler, sir. General Jack sent me over with a message."

"Well, don't just stand out there bellowing. Come on in."

The door edged open and the man stepped inside. "Major, sir," he said. "General Jack said to tell you that stoker wakened and he had a talk with him. Now he'd like to see this Devereaux feller in his office."

III

General Jack Casement's field office was a tent top without sidewalls. The general sat in a swivel chair behind a paper-littered desk under its shade. As Devereaux and the major walked toward him he struck a match to a thin black cigar. Then he eased back into the chair and looked curiously at Dev. There was a deep groove between his eyebrows, like a scowl-mark. But there were laughlines traced around his eyes. The groove might have come from squinting into the sharp sunlight of the plains.

He chewed on the cigar as he studied Dev. Finally he spoke: "Well, Mister Devereaux. I'll admit there was some question in my mind. We get some strange ones wandering around the railhead. But with that fireman's verification of your story, and with Major Nordstadt vouching for you. . . ." He held out a hand.

Dev tried not to let the sense of relief he felt show as he took the general's hand. "Thank you, sir," he said. It sounded stiff and a bit ridiculous.

The general was smiling pleasantly. "Exactly what happened last night?" The smile faded as he listened and when Dev had finished, he asked, "You didn't see anyone or anything?"

"No, sir. After the engine blew, I blacked out."

"Them damned Indians, I suppose," General Jack muttered.

"Indians?" Dev asked.

Major Nordstadt answered him. "They've plagued us all the way across the plains. We thought the worst of it was past, but since we've been here a small party has been pulling our spikes, digging our ties and taking snipes at the work crews. Now they've wrecked a train. . . ."

"It doesn't sound like Indians to me," Dev said.

Casement eyed him. "Why not?"

"Well, it just doesn't sound like the way Indians would work. Not pulling spikes."

"That Cheyenne, Turkey Leg, and his bunch wrecked one of our trains out near Plum Creek," General Jack told him. "He did it by pulling a joint loose and bending the rail. What makes you think this bunch isn't trying . . ." He stopped short, staring past Dev, and muttered, "What the hell?"

Dev looked back over his shoulder. Two track workers with rifles on their arms were hustling toward the tent. They were herding an Indian boy ahead of them.

"Well, speak of the devil. . . ." the general grunted. He called out, "What's going on?"

One of the track men shouted back: "General Jack, we've brought you a prisoner! They attacked us again, only this time we caught one!" He prodded at the boy with the muzzle of his gun.

As they told their story, Dev looked over the prisoner. He was young, maybe old enough to have been through his ordeal and made a warrior, but not by much. And from the look of him, he was a very frightened kid. His hands were tied behind him and he hunched his shoulders like a cornered animal.

When Casement called for someone who could speak with the boy, a burly worker in yellowleg britches stepped from the crowd that had gathered around the tent. He confronted the boy with a blast of syllables that set him to cowering. But he got no answer. Reddening around the neck, he raised a hand as if to slam it into the boy's face. "You'll answer me, you damned red . . ."

"Hold on," Dev snapped at him.

The yellowleg turned and stared at him with blazing eyes. "Who the hell are you to be buttin' in?"

"Name's Devereaux. And you won't get anything out of this boy by shouting at him in Cheyenne. He's Lakota."

The yellowleg frowned. "What do you know about it?"

"Plenty."

Casement asked, "Mister Devereaux, do you by some chance speak Sioux?"

"I can talk to him if you'll untie his hands."

The general nodded and ordered the boy untied. Then Dev stepped up and put a hand out, making a sweeping gesture from his own chest, then another. The boy's eyes followed and some of the fear eased out of his face. His own hands moved, gesturing so quickly that Dev had to slow him down to understand the sign talk. When he'd done, he told Casement, "It's just this kid's family raiding you. They're exiles from their tribe because his father broke a holy law."

"What about the raids? Why?"

"The boy says they've got a white friend who knows about railroads and who told them the rails are bad medicine. The friend told them the railroad will anger the buffalo and they'll all go away if it gets put through. He told them they could win honor and get themselves taken back by their tribe if they stop the railroad from coming through. But that's all he'll tell me."

The lines deepened between Casement's brows. "A *white* friend? Some damn renegade?" He looked toward the track workers and told them to take away the boy. Then he waved a hand at the crowd around the tent, shouting, "The rest of you get back

32

to your work or I'll dock the whole damn camp."

With a sudden murmuring and scurrying, they broke and raced away. But as Dev started to turn and follow, Casement called, "Not you, Devereaux."

Feeling the tension in his shoulders again, Dev turned back and faced him.

The general's eyes were probing. "A white renegade," he muttered to himself. Then he asked, "What's your line of work?"

"Buffalo hunting."

Casement took a last puff on the cigar and tossed away the butt. "That's good enough for openers. I think I could use you here at End-of-Track, Devereaux. Would you be interested in a job with the Union Pacific?"

Dev blinked and gazed at the general. His mouth twisted into a humorless grin. "I'm obliged for the offer, but I'm afraid I can't take you up on it."

"Why not?"

Slowly, he answered. "I'd like to, General, but I've got business up a ways that I have to take care of."

"Personal matter?"

He nodded.

"Yes," the general said. "Then I suppose you're anxious to be on your way?"

"Yessir!"

"Well, you're free to go. If you get your business settled or change your mind, I'd like to see you again."

"Thank you, sir," Dev stopped himself short of saluting. He turned and walked out of the open tent toward Major Nordstadt.

"Any trouble?" the major asked.

"No, I reckon not. He offered me a job."

"Now you . . ."

"Hey! Hey, you black Firbolg!" The girl's voice cut across the major's. "Hold up there in the Fitzpatrick's britches!"

She had her skirts gathered and was running toward them. Her brilliant red hair was tied at the nape of her neck, but loose strands of it flamed around her face, given light by the sun.

"Maury O'Neil!" the major called. "What are you doing bellowing like a lost locomotive?"

She came up breathlessly, laughing and frowning at the same time. "Ah, Major. It's this low, lying, thieving black-souled hide-skinner. He's wearing the Fitzpatrick's britches." She turned toward Dev and smiled, "It was a beautiful thing you did there, talking with your hands to that heathen. Would you teach me the art?"

He grinned back. "You'd take lessons

from a low, black Firbolg of a buffalo skinner?"

Her face reddened behind the freckles and twisted into a mocking scowl. "Oh, you — you — !" She shook her head as if that would help her find a suitable word. Then the scowl faded. She wrinkled her nose and shrugged. "Well now, you're not as foul smelling as you were, and I've a notion that with enough scrubbing you might eventually come clean. I've not as much hope for that hide shirt of yours, though. It's a vile thing that ought to be burnt. I've a mind to set the fire to it myself."

"You hold on there. You go burning my only shirt and your Fitzpatrick will never get this one back." He pulled at the gray flannel over his chest.

"Is that leather thing the *only* shirt you've got?"

He nodded.

She turned back to Major Nordstadt. "You see? You see what a miserable wretch this one is? Him with but one shirt to his name and that an old piece of animal skin that looks like he took it off a dead Indian and smells like he took it off a dead buffalo. I'm warning you, Major, no good'll come of him. I've a notion the only saving of him would be to put him onto honest work —

like maybe the laying of rail." Her tone was still mocking, but she turned her eyes down, unwilling for the major to see the seriousness of her suggestion in them.

The stern scowl he gave her was by no means serious. "Miss Maureen O'Neil, are you suggesting that I use my meager influence here to get this hide skinner a job with the Union Pacific?"

Now even her freckles seemed to be glowing red. "Well, sir, I expect it's the only chance of salvation he'll have. If he goes back to the buffalo range, he'll never get clean of the stink."

"I'm not going back to the buffalo," Dev said. "I'm going to Laramie."

She looked up then, her eyes wide and teasing. "Oh, bless you! That's even worse!"

"She might be right there, Dev," the major grinned.

"Well, right or wrong, it's where I'm going. And I reckon I'll be wearing the Fitzpatrick's britches if she doesn't give me back my own."

She planted her hands on her hips and gazed at him. "You're a worthless fool of a black-souled Firbolg and I can see I'm wasting my time even thinking of trying to help the likes of you. But if you'll follow along, I'll give you back your belongings." She spun on her heel and headed back toward her laundry lines with a long, swinging stride. As she reached them, she ducked and disappeared behind the waving rows of shirts.

When she reappeared, it was with Dev's clothes in her arms. "Here," she said, shoving them at him. "Take them and go to Laramie, if that's what you want."

"It's what I have to do," he answered. She really didn't want him to go, he thought. And he wished to hell he could stay. Taking the clothes, he muttered, "I'm obliged."

"We'll be seeing you again before you leave?" she asked, her golden eyes completely serious now.

He nodded and grinned. "Sure. I've got to return the Fitzpatrick's britches, haven't I?"

"Oh! Oh, you . . . !" Angrily she knotted one small fist and rammed it into his ribs. "You mock me, will you? You wretched creature!"

"Hey!" he grunted in surprise. "Hey, wait . . ." But she had dashed back under the clothesline and lost herself in the maze of laundry.

For a moment he stood with the bundle of clothes in his arms, staring at the line of wind-whipped shirts. Then he turned slowly and headed toward Major Nordstadt's waycar.

Like almost all of the furniture in the waycar, the commode was small and built-in. But even so, it was unaccustomed luxury for Dev. Noah had filled the basin and warmed it with boiling water for him when he stripped, and then disappeared. As he dipped a hand into the basin, he commented, "Those damn rivers on the buffalo range get colder'n a stockholder's heart."

The major was leaning back in his chair with his feet up on the bumper of the stove. He took the pipe out of his mouth and asked, "Is that where you learned the Indian sign talk?"

"That? No."

"It isn't something I'd have naturally expected of one of my telegraphists."

Dev grinned at his own image in the mirror. "You reckon I look like a white man, Major?" he asked.

Nordstadt studied him, frowning, and said, "Of course. Why?"

"Guess I take after Ma," he muttered. "You don't notice any sort of family resemblance between me and that Lakota boy back there?"

"What do you mean, Devereaux?"

"Well, I reckon we're not very close kin. He's fullblooded Lakota. I'm only quarter Siksiki. Blackfoot."

The major gazed at him speculatively, now seeing the bone of his face, the dark complexion and the dead black hair. "I could have sworn I recalled you being from New York City."

"That's where I lived when I enlisted," Dev answered. "But I was born and partly raised down around Bent's Old Fort. The kids I hung out with were mostly Blackfoot. And breeds like me. Didn't go East 'til I was twelve or thirteen."

"Where'd you get a name like Devereaux?"

"Grandpa. He was pure French. A mountain man — trapper by trade. He took up with the Siksika before Bent ever built his fort. Got himself killed thieving ponies from the Crow at the age of seventy-three."

"But your mother was a white woman?" the major asked.

Dev's grin faded. He looked deep into the mirror as if he were looking into a memory. "She was New York Dutch. Family of first settlers and rich as Midas' pig."

"Then you went to New York to your mother's people?"

"Kinda." Dev scrubbed at his face with

the towel, then put it down and turned toward the major. "With us Blackfeet, a child belongs to its mother's family, you know. Only *they* didn't figure it that way. After Pa died, Ma decided she ought to take me back East and raise me white. Only when we got to New York that family of hers wouldn't even see us. They'd disowned her for taking up with a breed. But by then we'd used up all the money we had and she was too sickly to make the trip back to Bent's. So we were stuck in New York with winter coming on."

"What did you do?"

"Found us a place of sorts. Down in Five Points. Only she died before the winter was out."

The major contemplated his boots. After a moment, he said, "Then you enlisted?"

"I kicked around on my own for a while first. I stoked for the N.Y. & H. for almost a year before I got to look old enough to talk my way into the army. Stoked for the U.S.M.R. a while too, before I got put to hammering a key in your office."

"When you came into my office, I was given to understand you were an experienced telegraphist."

Dev hesitated. He had the major's confidence and that was something he wasn't willing to lose. And he had a strong feeling that with the major it would be better to tell the truth about a lie than to try to hide it with more lies.

"Fact is, Major, I kinda misled a few people in getting assigned there," he said. "I'd been down with the fever for a while and I had a bunk mate from the telegraphists. He talked a lot and taught me the code. I always was kinda handy with my hands."

"Well now," the major grunted. He looked at Dev curiously. "I *thought* I knew the men in my office."

"Getting into the army was getting out of Five Points, Major. I never figured on going back there. Pounding brass was a good trade and I liked railroading. I had a notion once I got myself established in your office, I was set to rise in the world, if I had enough sense to keep myself out of trouble."

"And now you're trailing Danforth?"

"Not to *make* trouble. I mean to finish up trouble that's already been made. Devereaux was a good and respected name before I got hold of it. My name on that blacklist and those Pinks on my tail — I didn't earn that, Major, and I mean to change it."

Nordstadt nodded. "Then put on your britches and go on to Laramie. And keep in

41

touch with me. If you should need help. . . ."
He left it at that.

IV

For a while Dev followed the roadbed, but
when it curved behind a rise of land, he cut
across the brow of the slope. He halted on
the height, looking out at the basin. There
was a sprinkling of aspen and beyond it,
thick stands of fir rising up the mountain-
side.

Something was moving among the shad-
owed trees. A man — two men — both rifles
hooked at ready over their arms. They
seemed to be the same two who'd brought
the Indian boy to General Casement.

As Dev started toward them another flash
of motion caught his eye. There was someone hunched down behind a boulder in the
edge of the woods. Whoever it was, his back
was toward Dev with the boulder between
him and the hunters. His attention was
entirely on those two men stomping through
the trees. So that was what they were hunting, Dev thought as he watched.

Then one of the track workers spotted
Dev and sung out. They started toward him,
jogging awkwardly through the windfalls.
That was when the one behind the boulder

looked back and Dev saw that he was just a boy, with eyes that were like deep holes in his fear-whitened face. At the sight of that face, Dev moved quickly, passing by the hiding place and meeting the track layers. "What's the matter?" he asked them.

"Oh, it's you," one shouted back. And he saw that they were the ones he'd seen in camp. "You're the friend of General Jack's, ain't you?"

He nodded.

"Have you seen anything of a young feller in a butternut shirt scampering up this hill?" the man asked him.

"Why?" He glanced down at the Spencer in the worker's hand.

"He's been messing around the track. Looks like he was tampering with our spikes. Damned wrecker."

The image of the boy's pale face was vivid in Dev's mind. Slowly he said, "Maybe I seen him. Maybe I didn't. I saw something heading up that way at a pretty hard clip." He gestured in the far direction, away from the boulder where the boy hid. "Of course it might've been a pronghorn. They got a kinda butternut color."

"Oh, it was the lad all right," the worker said.

"No doubt," his companion agreed. "If

that's the way he went, we've lost him for sure. He musta doubled back on us."

The first man shrugged. "Well, we'd better get back and report this to General Jack." He mumbled a thanks to Dev and they both headed away hurriedly.

Dev stood waiting until they were out of sight around the slope and then some. When he felt certain they were gone, he turned toward the boulder and called: "You can come out now."

The boy slipped slowly from his hiding place. He was a nondescript youngster, tall and gangling, maybe sixteen or so. He gazed at Dev gratefully. "I'm sure thankful to you, mister. They'd have had my scalp for sure."

"*Were* you messing around the track?" Dev asked.

"Did they say *I* was doing that?" The boy looked at him wide-eyed. "It wasn't me. It was somebody else. Strangers. I come up on them and when they saw me they jumped on their horses and run off. I just stopped to see what they'd been doing when them two jayhawks come along and started shooting at me. So I lit out and hid." He tumbled the words out hurriedly — as if he'd stored them up in his head and had to spill them out before he lost some of them. He had an open face and his eyes held steady as he spoke. But they were strange eyes — flat and unrevealing. As he scanned Dev's clothes, he said, "I sure thank you, mister. You ain't with the railroad, are you?"

"No."

"I didn't think so. I don't reckon nobody with the railroad would have helped me out that way."

"You live around here?" Dev asked.

"Over a ways toward Laramie." The boy looked at him questioningly.

"Got a mount, or are you afoot?"

"My pony's down yonder."

"Let's get it then. I'm seeing you home."

For a moment the boy looked as if he were going to protest. Then he turned and led Dev through the woods to a small ravine where a sorrel pony was tied in the brush. It was well hidden. The boy untied the reins and climbed into the saddle. Doubtfully, he said, "We can ride double, I reckon."

Dev swung up behind him and he laid heels to the pony. It wasn't long before they raised sight of the place.

It was a farm. A shallow basin between twinned ridges had been cleared, broken and, at some time past, planted. And once the house and barn had been painted, but now only patches and flakes of yellowed white-lead clung to the weathered walls.

As they rode across the muddy, weed-grown fields, a man appeared in the doorway of the barn. His hand rested on the butt of the revolver he wore at his side, as he watched them approach. After a moment he called out, "Asa, who's that with you?" His accent struck Dev as familiar. Illinois?

"A stranger, Paw," the kid answered. "Not a railroader. Wait'll I tell you what happened."

The old man stepped out to meet them and Asa drew rein. He spilled out his story just as he'd recited it for Dev — almost word for word. When he'd finished the old man looked up at Dev, studying him intently. His face was gaunt, with deep creases around the eyes and there was no trace of humor in them. The eyes were like the boy's — flat and secretive.

"I'm Jube Engels," he said. "Climb down and rest yourself."

Dev swung off the pony and extended his hand. Jube did not take it.

Glancing up at the sun, the old man said, "My woman'll be setting the table afore long. You're welcome to join us if you want." From the tone of his voice, it was a grudging invitation.

But Devereaux found he had a strong curiosity about this man and his blank-faced son. He wanted to know just why the boy had been down there at the track. "I'd be obliged," he answered.

With a jerk of his head, Engels ordered his son to go tell his woman there'd be a guest at dinner. Then he turned toward Dev and mumbled, "I gotta get back to work. You set and rest yourself if you want." With that, he ducked back into the barn.

As Dev walked toward the house, he looked around, wondering if this was the same man who'd built this farm or if he'd acquired it from some more industrious former owner. It seemed to have been a right nice place once. He decided to settle on the porch steps, in the warm patch of sunlight there. With his head back against a post, he closed his eyes.

Alarm! Somebody was beating the fire-gong. He jerked his eyes open and glanced around quickly. Not an alarm but a dinner call. A woman was standing on the porch not far from him, beating against the sounding iron that hung from a rafter. She turned her eyes toward him for a moment.

There was nothing of welcome or even acknowledgement in her look. It settled on him as listlessly as if he'd been something as common as the family hound dozing on the steps. Then she turned and walked back into the house.

As he got to his feet, Dev saw Jube Engels coming out of the barn. The old man was heading for the house, striding rapidly, his heels pounding against the earth as if he were marching toward some vital goal. It was the walk of a determined and confident man who'd made his plans in the world and would fight to achieve them. It didn't fit with the seedy, chaw-eared state of the farm. Coming up to the steps, Jube assembled his face into a smile of sorts and led Dev on into the house.

One of the women working at the fireplace was the gaunt creature he'd seen on the porch. The other was a girl, maybe a year or two older than Asa. Her cornsilk yellow hair was drawn into a loose knot at the nape of her neck. It was the fine, wispy hair of a child's, but her body under the homespun she wore was full womanly.

As Dev looked at her, she turned toward him and her eyes met his. They were purple-blue, like the lupine blossoms. In a quick, scanning glance, she looked from his face to his shoulders, down his body and at his face again, now with approval in her eyes. For an instant her lips hinted a smile. Then she turned away.

He heard the door swing open and looked

around as Asa came in with another man. The boy said, "This here is my brother, Lige."

The introduction wasn't necessary. Lige's face was his label. He looked a few years older than Asa and there was a scruff of yellow whiskers on his jaw, but his eyes and the bone of his face were the same as the boy's. He nodded to Dev as he took his place at the table.

When they all were settled, with their plates in front of them, Jube bowed his head and steepled his fingers.

"God," he said as bruskly as if he were addressing a visiting drummer, "we're obliged to You for all the good things You've give us. But of recent You've been putting hard times on our poor heads. If we've sinned again' You, we repent it. But if You've sent these plagues on us to test us like You did Job, well Sir, we'll fight 'em. And by thunder, we'll lick 'em! We'll drive them back to the Devil where they belong! Amen."

The family echoed the *amen* and Jube reached for a biscuit.

Asa retold his story, again in almost the same words he'd first told. Nobody commented and for the most part the meal was eaten in silence. It was a heavy, ill-fitting silence and Dev felt that it was because of his presence. The Engels men seemed to have things to say to each other that they were unwilling to speak of in front of a stranger, so they said nothing. When the meal was finished they pushed back their chairs and as he built himself a smoke, Lige finally spoke up. Eying Dev, he asked, "Where you headed?"

"Laramie."

"Afoot?" Jube asked, and he nodded in reply.

"Why afoot? In these parts a man should have a horse."

"I reckon he should," Dev agreed.

"We got a few head of saddle stock," Jube told him. "Seeing what you done for my boy there, I'd be willing to let you have one at a good price."

"I ain't afoot of choice," Dev answered. "Right now I'm kinda out of money."

"You figure on working in Laramie?"

He nodded.

"Why don't you try hiring on with the railroad?" Lige suggested. Or was it a suggestion? There was something curious in the tone of his voice. Something hostile?

As if he were making a reluctant admission, Dev said, "The railroad and I ain't none too friendly toward each other."

"Is that so?" Jube leaned forward, interested. "What did they do to you?"

"It isn't anything worth talking about." Dev shrugged.

The old man sat back, studying him speculatively. "Well, I'll tell you, Devereaux. You look like an honest Christian to me. I'd consider letting you take a horse on your note."

"The piebald?" Lige asked and his father nodded.

"Would you be interested?" Jube pressed.

"I might be," Dev said, keeping his voice noncommital. It was expected of a prospective buyer.

Lige ground out the cigarette butt in his plate and got to his feet. "She's in the corral. I'll show her to you." With his father, he headed out the door.

As Dev started after them, the girl stepped around him, reaching for a plate on the table. She brushed against his arm, and he muttered, "Sorry."

She smiled. "Paw likes you." Her voice was high and thin. "He likes anybody who don't like the railroad. He'd welcome you if you was to come back again." The lupine eyes were boldly inviting and she brushed against him again as she reached for another plate.

Without making any answer to her, he headed for the door. He heard Jube and Lige on the porch, exchanging quick, hushed words. Jube was saying, "Damned fool boy, trying to do it by his lonesome. I'll tar him good if he tries it again . . ."

As Dev stepped through the door they cut their words short and Lige told him, "Come on, and I'll show you the horse."

It was a shaggy tobiano mare, gaunt of rib and hammerheaded with a goose rump but a full chest and good legs. As Dev came up on her near side she shied away from him, swinging her head around in his direction. For an instant he thought she was going to lunge and try to sink her teeth into him. But she just stood, looking full-face at him.

"She's blind in the left eye," he said to Lige.

"No, she ain't. She's just squaw-broke. Try her from the other side."

Dev walked around and approached her from the right. She stood headhung as he leaned his arms on her back. He agreed, "She's squaw-broke, all right but she's still blind in one eye." As he crossed in front of her, she turned her head, craning her neck as he stepped up to her left flank.

Lige frowned in apparent disbelief.

"Pull her head around and I'll show you,"

Dev said.

Lige took hold of the halter and tugged it until he'd straightened her neck. Then Dev raised a hand and brought it toward her head from behind, as if he meant to hit her. She didn't flinch. With a nod, he repeated, "Blind."

"Well, I'll be damned," Lige mumbled a little too incredulously. "I didn't have no idea of that. I just figured she was shy on account of being Indian broke."

"She ain't worth much," Dev suggested.

"She's a good breeding horse," was Lige's protest. "Look at the legs and chest on her."

"I'm looking at the head and rump."

They dickered a while over her points and her price and finally settled. Dev signed a note with a promise to pay or return the horse with a little boot for its hire. He managed to get a snaffle-bit plow bridle thrown in on the deal, but the Engels didn't have a saddle they were willing to part with for less than cash. So he swung up onto the pony's bare back. Sitting aft of her sharp withers, he nudged her with his spurs and headed her along the trail toward Laramie.

V

The sun was hunkering low over the western horizon and the false-fronted buildings along the main street of Laramie cast long shadows when Dev reached them. But nothing on the street seemed to close down at twilight. Windows spilled yellow lamplight into the shadows and shopkeepers were setting out lanterns for their customers.

The Indian pony perked its ears and sniffed at the mixed odors of animals, men, and whiskey. It swung its head, warily studying the town through its one good eye, and took mincing sidesteps through the fetlock-deep mud that wheels and hooves had churned out of the street. Like the pony, Dev felt the excitement of the town. Eagerly, he scanned the people on the walks, hoping to catch sight of Danforth.

And suddenly he became aware that someone was watching him. He found the staring eyes in the crowd. It was an Indian — more likely a blanket breed from the look of him. He wore a long red-tipped feather in the band of his black Kossuth hat, and clutched a faded trade goods blanket around his shoulders. When Dev looked back at him, he slipped into the crowd and disappeared somewhere within it.

Dev nudged the pony on, toward the heart of the jerry-built town. A big imitation stucco false-front dominated the corner just ahead and the sturdy timber structure behind it looked an honest two stories high. On either side of the batwing doors were windows with panes of glass in them. By the lanternlight, Dev read the lettering on the windows: *Bannerman's Grand Palace.*

Major Nordstadt had said that Danforth hung out in a place called the *Palace.*

He glanced over the men who loitered around the windows and drifted through the doors. A blanketed figure with a feather in its black Kossuth hat leaned against the door jamb.

From the corner of his eye, Dev watched the Indian stir himself and slip through the batwings. With a flick of the reins, he brought the pony up to the hitchrail and slid off. He started to follow the Indian, then hesitated, putting a foot up on the plank walk. He bent and unbuckled one spur, then the other. He wiped them against his pantsleg and studied them under the lantern light. Not very fancy, but good serviceable spurs.

Pushing through the batwings, he stepped into the din and stench of the saloon. The *Palace* was no ordinary fly-by-night tent-saloon. It looked like this Bannerman, whoever he was, had built with the intention of staying on here in Laramie awhile. The bar was massive, the beams and rafters were set solid, and the walls were papered. A staircase with a narrow landing halfway up it, ran to the second floor, and the banister was carved mahogany.

Scanning the crowd, Dev picked out a couple of Kossuth hats, but none with red-tipped feather in the band. He edged his way on through to the bar and slapped his spurs down on it. A sandy-moustached bartender glanced at them and eyed Dev suspiciously.

"How much?" Dev asked.

The bartender picked up one spur and turned it in his hands, squinting at it as if he were studying a diamond that had been offered up for pawn. He dropped it carelessly on the bar — the diamond had turned out to be paste. In a cold flat voice, he said: "Two bits."

"Like hell," Dev muttered, putting his hand over them as if to pick them up. "They're worth easy two dollars — gold."

The bartender laughed. "You'd be robbing me at two bits."

Wearily, Dev leaned an elbow on the bar. He figured they'd settle for around six bits in hard money. That was about what the spurs would be worth. But getting the price for them would be a job of jaw work. He began to praise their virtues. The bartender made his answers, and finally they settled. Grumbling, the bartender paid, and Dev ordered a beer. The man was still grumbling when he set it down in front of him.

He leaned forward as he picked it up, intending to ask about Danforth. But as he raised the mug, someone slammed into his shoulder. The beer splashed over his hand and onto the bar.

He jerked around, looking for the man who'd jostled him, sensing that it had been done intentionally. He found himself looking into deep brown eyes set under heavy black brows that almost met over a short, straight nose. They were friendly, good-natured eyes, set in a full, boyish face.

The black-browed man grinned, his lips spreading back over white teeth. For an instant, it looked as though he were going to apologize for a mistake. Then the grin turned into a sneer. The man sniffed and looked past Dev, to the bartender who'd taken a sudden interest. Loudly, he said, "Something in here sure as hell stinks."

Why me, Dev wondered as he carefully set down the mug. He wiped his beer-spattered knuckles against the leg of his pants. In a soft, level voice, he said, "I don't have a gun on me."

Black-brow looked puzzled. He asked, "What's that supposed to mean?"

Dev sighed. "If you're looking for a killing, you're out of luck. If you'll settle for a fistfight, we'll need more elbow room."

The man studied him incredulously for a moment, then grinned again. "It's too mucky in the street. How about over there under the stairs?"

Dev glanced into the backbar mirror. He could see a clear space of sorts under the landing. Turning, he pushed his way toward it with black-brow close behind him. Over his shoulder he asked, "Why?"

"Hell, why not?" the grinning man said. With a shrug he added, "Sides, it's my job."

"Fighting me?"

As if it were an answer, the man told him, "I'm Hal Jarrett."

"Is that supposed to mean something to me?" Dev said. They'd come into the clear area now and he was able to get a better look at this fellow. A flash dandy, he thought as he looked over the black suit, the white linen shirt and the wide-brimmed felt hat that sat well back on Jarrett's curly black hair. The boyish face was clean-shaven and as fresh-scrubbed as if he were on his way to Sunday meeting.

Jarrett took off the hat and set it down carefully. Then he bent and unlashed the tie-down that held his holster. Dev glanced at the butt of the Colt Navy. It was darkened and worn to a high polish from handling.

As he straightened up, Jarrett eyed Dev. "You're kinda rushing into this, ain't you?" he asked suspiciously.

Dev's voice was dully patient. "I've already bargained to buy a horse and to sell my spurs today. I'm weary with dickering. I don't know why I'd gotta fight you, but if I have to, let's get it done with."

Jarret grinned again. He seemed oddly pleased. Facing Dev, he crouched slightly and lunged.

Dev sidestepped with a light, easy motion and brought up a fist that caught him just under the ribs. He staggered back with a grunt like a bull buffalo. Catching his balance he hesitated, sizing Dev up, then charged again. He threw a fist and Dev blocked it with his forearm, driving his other hand up under the arm, ramming Jarret in the belly again.

Flailing, Jarrett swung a clenched fist into Dev's shoulder, throwing him off balance for an instant. He followed it quickly, his left slamming into Dev's chest. Jarrett wasn't especially big, but he was built solid and there was more weight behind his punches than Dev had expected. Stumbling back, Dev managed to keep his feet.

Jarrett tried to close but again Dev caught his blow with a forearm and drove under the arm. Jarrett doubled over, clutching his arms against his body, then rose suddenly driving for Dev's stomach. But Dev spun, sidestepping away, at the same time lashing out, catching Jarrett with a quick rabbit punch, following with a solid blow that sent him sprawling toward the wall.

Leaning on his shoulder, Jarrett gulped deep breaths. Dev didn't press. Instead, he wiped the back of his hand across his mouth and flexed the muscles of his hands and arms, taking advantage of the momentary pause. He was weary, hungry and still haunted by aches from the wreck the night before. He needed the moment's rest as much as Jarrett.

Suddenly Jarrett rushed, intending to land a fist in Dev's belly. But Dev anticipated him, twisting on one foot and bringing a fist down hard into Jarrett's kidney. At that, Jarret wheeled, swinging wildly. His fist caught Dev across the jaw, jerking his head back, sending sparks of pain shooting up behind his eyes. The taste of salt filled his mouth.

Blindly, he drove a fist in Jarrett's direction. It was caught by an outthrust arm, fended off. But Dev's other hand had followed. It came under the arm, slamming into Jarrett's midsection. Again, Jarrett broke away, gasping for breath.

Dev shook his head, trying to clear his vision, and Jarrett swung for his head. Knuckles rammed into Dev's cheek as he tried to duck the blow. He lashed out, openhanded and upward. The back edge of his hand snapped against Jarrett's throat, and Jarrett staggered, falling back and coughing.

He hadn't caught his breath yet, when he dove for Devereaux again. He lunged, ramming out with one hand, then the other. But the blows weren't as strong as they should have been. Dev closed with him then, slamming his fists like the pistons of an engine into the soft flesh of Jarrett's belly, hearing his grunts like the exhausting of steam. Jarrett thrashed, his weakening blows falling at random.

Something butted into the small of Dev's back. Something hard and cold, and he heard the click of a gunhammer being cocked. A flat, chill voice rasped into his ear: "Stop it. Let him go."

Dev straightened, his fists easing open.

Jarrett staggered back, leaning against the wall and clutching his hands to his stomach. Dev raised his hands as the gun nuzzled harder into his spine. He asked wearily, "You always win this way?"

Jarrett's chest heaved as he struggled breath into his lungs. He raised a hand to brush at the damp hair that hung on his forehead. His eyes met Dev's and he grinned. Breathlessly, he said, "It beats losing." Then he looked past Dev questioningly.

Dev heard the voice again — a cold voice like stone grating on stone. "Ruby said to stop it."

Jarrett was breathing more easily now. He raised an eyebrow and shrugged slightly. "It was *my* fight. You hadn't ought to have butted in."

"You questioning my orders, Hal?" It was a woman who spoke.

Dev looked up. She stood on the landing with her hands resting on the rail. As she leaned over and looked down at the men, her eyes settled on Dev. She reminded him of a painting he'd seen somewhere — a Spanish Dona on a balcony. Her dress was green velvet that showed her shoulders smooth and soft. The hair piled on her head and tumbling down those ivory shoulders in carefully formed curls was red — not the flaming copper of Maury O'Neil's, but a rich dark chestnut. It framed a face as perfectly formed and flawless as a fine cameo.

"Bring him up here," she said. It was in her tone that she was accustomed to giving orders. It was in the toss of her head, too, as she turned away.

Jarrett led the way up the stairs and toward a door that stood open. At it, he stepped aside, ducking his head in a mock bow as the gunman nudged for Dev to go on in.

The room was an office. A flattopped desk faced the door and the woman was seated at it. A whale oil lamp, its cut glass bowl and bright brass sparkling, cast a ring of warm light on the mahogany desk top and on the woman's cameo face as she looked up at Devereaux. It was an expensive lamp and she — well, she looked accustomed to luxury.

Her eyes were green. They caught the light like cut crystals. She pursed her lips slightly as she studied Dev. "Who are you?" she asked and there was no tone of authority in her voice now. It was soft, husky.

"A buffalo skinner."

"What do they call you?"

"Dev."

"How long have you been in Laramie?"

"How long did that fight take?"

She looked past him at the man with the gun and raised an eyebrow in question. "Why a buffalo hunter?"

Jarrett appeared within Dev's field of vision. He'd stripped off his shirt and was walking to the commode in the corner. As he picked up the pitcher and began to fill the basin, he said, "This feller rode in on that calico mare of Engels'. The Breed saw him ride in. Knowing how Dolph feels about Engels . . ."

"So you decided to take action in Dolph's behalf."

"Hell, Ruby. I know Dolph wouldn't have an Engels in this place and if this one is working for them then he's no better'n them."

She turned back to Dev. "Where did you get the calico horse?"

"Engels. I bought it from him."

Jarrett grunted skeptically. "You *bought* that blind old nag? *Bought* that miserable hack when there's good sound mesteñas to be had for damned near nothing?" He looked at the woman and asked, "Who'd be riding that nag except he'd hired on for Engels and that was what the old man gave

64

him to ride?"

She looked to Dev for an answer.

"Next to nothing isn't the same as nothing," he said. "I came onto the Engels place afoot and busted. The old man was willing to sell me that horse on my note to pay. If I could have gotten a sound bronc on the same terms I'd have taken it." He started a hand toward his pocket, but hesitated at the nudge of the gun against his spine.

The woman's eyes had followed his hand and there was a hint of amusement in them. He saw it. Ignoring the gun, he thrust his hand into the pocket and brought out a folded scrap of paper. When he held it out, she took it from him and thumbed it open with a long, tapered nail. She scanned it and, turning toward Jarrett, said, "It's a bill of sale from Jube Engels and a promise to pay."

Jarrett grinned. "My mistake, I reckon," he said genially. He dipped a towel into the basin and pressed it against his stomach, wincing slightly at the touch.

Ruby glanced at the bill of sale again. "It's in the name of Devereaux."

"Dev for short."

"French?" she asked.

"Partly."

"You aren't from New Orleans?"

65

"No."

"Too bad," she murmured. For an instant her deep green eyes seemed to look far past him. "I met Dolph in New Orleans. That was a long time ago — before the war. It's a wonderful place, New Orleans. All the lights — the places and the clothes and . . ."

"Any time, Ruby. We can go there any time you say the word." That was the voice of the gunman, but it was no longer as cold as stone.

Her eyes frosted over. "All right Stark," she said. "You can put away that revolver now."

Dev felt the gun muzzle withdrawn from the small of his back and was aware of the man stepping away from him. Ruby smiled and looked at Dev a little like a person might scan a horse he anticipated buying. She asked, "You're looking for work?"

He nodded.

"Can you do anything besides skin buffalo?" she asked.

"What do you want done?" he said. He was aware of the quick, curious glance that Jarrett shot him.

Ruby stood up. She walked around the desk and faced him as if she were measuring herself against him. Then she turned and walked out of the circle of lamplight.

66

When she faced him again, he could not see her eyes. Her voice was businesslike. "Dolph and I do some freighting. He lets me handle the freight line. I'll hire you. Dollar and a half a day and found. You'll get your food and bed here at the *Palace*."

"Damnit, Ruby. . . ." For the first time, the stone-voiced gunman stepped within Dev's sight. He was a tall, spare man — the kind who seems as if the fires in him burn the flesh off his bones and keep him gaunt as a snake. His hands moved restlessly as he spoke in whispers to the woman. He took her by the arm and drew her away from the desk, and Dev couldn't make out their words, but from the dancing of his hands he was angry. And from the way Ruby tossed her head, she was annoyed.

Dev shifted his weight, feeling uncomfortable at standing there while they argued. And he was hungry and tired.

Jarrett had pulled on his shirt again. As he tucked in the tails, he called softly, "Devereaux." He gestured for Dev to come along as he headed for the door. Quietly, he said, "You fill your belly downstairs while those two are fighting. And Ruby'll find you when she wants you. You've got no worry about that."

When Jarrett had got good and loosened

up, Devereaux led the conversation to include the inhabitants of Hell-on-Wheels. In particular he led the conversation to include the whereabouts of Charlie Danforth. Trying to keep his voice steady despite the beer that was beginning to affect him, he asked: "Say, there *is* someone around here I might know. Maybe you've heard of him — feller named Charlie Danforth."

Well likkered up as he was, Jarrett had been quick enough to catch the strain in Dev's voice.

"Where you know Charlie Danforth from?"

"Illinois, if it's the same feller. You know him? Is he around here?"

"You ask that easy enough, I reckon, but you're too tense. You've got some real good reason for asking about Charlie. Maybe you even came to Laramie 'specially to find him." It was a question.

"Maybe I did," Dev snapped, angry at himself for having let Jarrett read so much of his thoughts. "You know where he is?"

"Is it on account of a woman that you're hunting him? That's what usually caused him trouble. He make free with your woman?"

"No. You gonna give me an answer, Jarrett? You know where Danforth is?"

"If it weren't a woman, what was it?"

"None of your damned business!" Dev shouted. "You know where he is or don't you?"

A corner of Jarrett's mouth had twisted slightly then, but he wasn't smiling. "Sure. You'll find him up the hill a ways." His eyes were steady on Devereaux, probing as he spoke. "Him and Johnny Stark had a sort of falling out yesterday. We buried him this morning."

The rest of the night's activities were just vague memories. And every once in a while Devereaux would recall Jarrett's words telling him that Charlie Danforth was dead. That had hit hard.

VI

Devereaux rolled over and stretched out an arm across the double bed. His hand found only the other pillow. He became aware of the dull throbbing in his head and the thick, slimy taste in his mouth. He lay still, trying to come fully awake, trying to remember why he'd gotten drunk.

After dinner he and Jarrett had set in to do a little serious drinking together.

And then he remembered a woman! He

could recall the softness of her shoulders, the feel of her under his hands, the heat of her mouth against him. He could remember the deep crystal green of her eyes — hot, hungry eyes. Ruby Bannerman?

He became aware of the strange feel of the pillow under his hand. It was soft and smooth. Forcing his eyes open, he focused on it. There was sunlight filtering through the curtained window, giving a sheen to the white satin pillowslip. Satin? Curtains?

He looked around the room. It was a lot bigger than the cubbyhole of Hal Jarrett's. There was an upholstered chair, the seat piled with a crumple of green velvet and white lace. There was a big mirror, reflecting a mahogany dresser with a crystal-prismed lamp on it, and a door. As he gazed at the reflection, the door opened.

He rolled over, one hand automatically reaching for the carbine he'd kept at his side on the buffalo range. His hand closed on bedcovers.

The man who stepped through the door halted as if he'd been drawn up on a Spanish bit. He looked at Dev, his forehead creasing into a frown. He was very blond, with hair the creamy white of an albino and almost translucent skin, but he hadn't the tall bony build. His shoulders were uncommonly wide for a short man, and he filled out his suit as if his bones were well-plated with muscle. He studied Dev through ice-blue eyes.

Aware that he was stone naked, Dev clutched the bedcovers against his chest with one hand as he sat up. He glanced around, saw his clothes in a heap on the floor with the Colt Dragoon half-buried under them. It was well out of reach.

The man in the doorway was no longer scowling. His face was as blank as his voice when he spoke. "You're the new man Ruby hired?"

Wordlessly, Dev nodded.

"Get dressed and meet me downstairs," the man said. He turned and started back through the door, then glanced at Dev and added, "I'm Dolph Bannerman, Ruby's husband!"

Dev leaned out of bed and grabbed the Colt. With it in his hand, he looked back at the clothes heaped on the chair. *Ruby Bannerman's husband! What the hell. . . .*

As he dressed he kept the revolver close at hand. Then he buckled on the gunbelt and tried slipping the Dragoon quickly out of the holster. He'd handled guns often enough, amused himself at Willis Siding by practicing with a handgun. But now the mo-

71

tion was awkward, his hand unsteady. His head ached and he rubbed at his burning eyes with the back of his hand as he cursed his image in the mirror. Then he started downstairs.

The saloon was closed but one lamp in the back puddled light down onto a single occupied table. The two men seated there were Dolph Bannerman and Hal Jarrett. The scent of the fried ham and eggs on the table stirred a feeling of nausea in Dev's stomach, and Bannerman's cold nod didn't help matters any.

Jarret glanced at him and grinned. "Breakfast, Dev. Coosie's in a good mood this morning. The food's almost fit to eat." He gestured for Dev to pull up a chair.

"Just coffee," Dev muttered as he sat down.

Hal laughed. "Old friend, we sure showed Hell-on-Wheels a few twists last night, didn't we? Showed 'em what a couple of Texans can do when they put their minds to it."

"You from Texas?" Bannerman asked Dev conversationally.

Hal answered for him. "Being a Texan ain't a matter of nationality. It's a state of mind. Dev here is almost as Texican as I am. Only he don't seem to bear up as well next morning."

Dev tried to return his grin. "I'm a mite out of practice. It gets kinda dry on the buffalo range sometime."

"Well, we'll get you back into practice around here. Ain't no place in the world damper with corn-dew than Laramie." He forked a cut of egg into his mouth and chewed with enthusiasm.

Bannerman took over the conversation. "Hal tells me you're a hide hunter by trade."

"That's what I've been working at."

"Looks to me like there's good money in buffalo. I've been giving some thought to outfitting a crew or two and sending them onto the range."

"I'm not too interested in going after the bulls again," Dev muttered.

Bannerman said, "You might give it some thought. Hang around Laramie if you want. I've decided to settle here. When it's time to start outfitting, you can give me your answer. I figure to pay a commission, so if you're any good you'd stand to profit well by it."

"Sounds like a good deal to me," Hal put in.

Dev made himself grin again. "Would you fancy going out on the range with me?"

"Hell no! I got a trade and I'm happy

working at it. I like the city life."

"I couldn't spare Hal," Bannerman told him. "He's one man I can trust." He finished his coffee and stood up. "Well, Devereaux, Hal can show you around. If there's anything you need, he'll introduce you at the mercantile and you can draw on our account against your wage."

Once he was gone, Dev leaned toward Hal and asked softly, "Do you know where I was last night?"

"You was with me," Hal answered, his face innocent.

"You know damned well what I mean."

He nodded, not meeting Dev's eyes.

Dev leaned back and stared into his coffee. He said, "Bannerman knows."

For a long moment Hal gazed into the distance, as if he were examining a variety of thoughts. Then he said, "As long as you treat Ruby decent, you got nothing to worry about from Dolph."

"God, man! Don't you understand . . ." Dev realized that Hal did understand — that Hal knew and understood far more than he himself. Incredulously, he asked, "Doesn't he *care?*"

"You think you're the first one?" Hal said. "Before you there was Stark and before him there was me and before that Danforth.

Sure, Dolph cares but . . . hell, you just treat Ruby decent and don't nose around too much. You're too damned serious-minded. You'll be better off if you take what comes and don't try to know too much. It ain't Dolph you've got to worry about. It's Stark."

"Hal, I've got a right to know. . . ."

"There's some things no man has a right to know about another man," Jarrett interrupted, his voice harshly serious. He leaned back, studying his knuckles for a moment. "I got one failing, Devereaux. I'm too damned curious. I nose around til I find out all kinds of things I shouldn't. I get away with it partly because I got a fast hand with a gun and partly because I got a grin like an idiot.

"Folks take my gun serious but they can't help thinking otherwise I'm sort of harmless. You ain't got nothing like that working for you. Your gun ain't fast enough and you don't look like a fool. You'll end up with a ball through your gut and *that's* none of my damned business either." He slapped his hand down flat on the table. The sound of it cut through the room like a gunshot.

He got to his feet and strode across the room, his bootheels hammering on the planks. Dev watched as he pushed open the door and stepped outside.

Alone in the silence, Dev stared at his own thoughts. Hal had warned him at least twice now to look out for Stark, and Stark had gunned Danforth. What had their argument been? What argument did Stark have with *him?* Ruby Bannerman?

He rested his head in his hands and asked himself how the hell he'd gotten involved with Ruby Bannerman?

The patches of sunlight on the floor moved and the coffee in the cup grew cold. But Dev wasn't aware of how much time had passed when the door swung open and he heard Hal Jarrett's cheery voice.

"Dev, old friend, you shoulda seen it. There's some folks down the road what keep this she-goat and it got loose this morning. It lit out up the road just when Ron Archer come driving up in his red wheeled wagon with the little sorrel mare 'tween the sticks. Old nanny goat come straight under the mare's belly. Mare went up on her hind haunches, busted her leathers and lit a shuck for Texas. Left Ron setting them on the box all by his lonesome. And to top it, damned if Old Nan didn't take a flying leap and land herself whomp in his lap.

"Well, Ron's got himself a set of them billygoat chin whiskers and they musta looked right handsome to Old Nan because she just sets there and starts nibbling on them, slobbering her tongue all over Ron's face and making up to him like he's the fanciest thing in britches she's seen this side of the Arkansas." He slapped a hand against his thigh and doubled over, laughing. "Damnit, Dev, you shoulda seen it. Oh, he ain't gonna live this down easy. It's been *Ron* up to now, but after this it's gonna be *Billy* for him!"

He bent with laughter again, then caught his breath and clapped a hand on Dev's shoulder. "What say we wander out and see what else is going on around town? Maybe you want to stop by the mercantile and look for something to spend your wages on?"

Dev trailed along with him into the morning sunlight. Shading his eyes with his hand, he muttered, "I reckon I could use a hat. And maybe a new shirt."

Hal was still chewing his twist of licorice when they got back to the room. He sprawled on the bed while Dev washed and changed into the new clothes he'd bought. He watched critically as Dev studied himself in the mirror.

Dev brushed at the store creases in the shirt and wondered what Maury O'Neil would think about it. Would she be impressed by him having a new shirt, a horse and a gun as well? Or would she mock him for the shirt being linsey-woolsy and the horse being half blind?

Hal finished off the licorice and commented, "That's a fool look on your face. Does it mean anything?"

Embarrassed at being caught in such thoughts, Dev glanced around. His eyes stopped on the window. The sun was well up. He said, "I was just thinking how I've been spending money I ain't earned yet. I sure ought to get over to that freight office and see what my job is."

With a sigh, Hal swung his legs off the bed and sat up. "If you're so itchy to get working, go ahead. I'm going down to the kitchen and see what Coosie's got in mind for dinner." He slapped his hat on his head, brim down over his face and tromped out.

Dev grinned at the door. The idea of work seemed to make Hal a mite uneasy. He turned back to the mirror and fiddled with the new scarf a bit, then squared the felt hat up and walked out.

He found the freightyard easy enough. It was quiet. A few head of harness stock drowsed in the corral and a blacksmith tinkered around the forge across the yard from the main shack. Dev stepped into the office and introduced himself to the man at the desk.

"Nobody told *me* there was a new driver," the agent snapped back at him. "Can you prove you've been hired on here?"

Dev was taken aback by the question. But before he could frame an answer someone spoke from behind him.

"I'll vouch for him." The voice was stony hard.

Dev wheeled. He hadn't heard anyone come in, but there was Stark, standing at his shoulder and smiling thinly. With a nod to Dev, Stark said, "Devereaux here got himself hired on last night by Ruby. If he wants a wagon give him a wagon."

Scowling, the agent insisted, "Ruby Bannerman is boss, but I got no wagons. Even if I had a wagon, I got no loads."

Stark considered. He asked, "What about Nash's place? Ain't you got a trip down there now?"

"I might have some stuff," the agent admitted reluctantly. "But that's two days out and two days back. I figured I'd give it to Tucker tomorrow."

"Hell, it ain't a day and a half easy way, even if you drive slow," Stark said. "Tucker takes so long on account of he has to sober up before he can start back. You send

79

Devereaux and he'll show you how he can cover ground. Prove himself a real asset to the firm. Make Ruby right happy . . ." He grinned slightly as he let his voice trail off.

The agent sighed. "All right. It's an easy trip," he told Dev. "You might run into a few redskins but for the most part they're friendly. They trade at Nash's themselves. Tame Arapahoe mostly."

"What about the Sioux?" Dev asked.

"They won't bother you," Stark snapped. "Bannerman says he and his got no worry from them."

Bannerman said? Did he know those Lakota, Dev wondered. The boy had spoken of a white friend. He turned his thoughts back to the job, asking directions to Nash's trading post. When he'd gotten them and a note of introduction to Nash, the agent issued him a rifle.

"Hope I won't need this," he said, hefting the new Spencer repeater.

"Don't you worry about that," Stark said. "Don't you worry about nothing."

"You just take out the supplies to Nash and bring back the trade payment," the agent said. "And make sure the load you bring back checks the bill of lading he gives you or you'll answer to Bannerman."

"Yes," Stark muttered. He was grinning as

if he were enjoying some private joke — at Dev's expense. "And you'll be back in three or four days, I reckon."

Dev drove out of Laramie feeling apprehensive about Stark's attitude. It just didn't make sense — the way Stark had vouched for him and then grinned. But the trip to Nash's was uneventful. It went quickly and, in fact, was downright pleasant.

Driving back, he made better time than he'd dared hope. He decided he had enough time to detour by way of End-of-Track and make his night camp there. He wanted to see and talk to Major Nordstadt again. When he thought of Maury O'Neil, he tried to tell himself she wasn't his reason for wanting to go back. Still, it would be nice to see her again.

The sun was gone and the moon had begun to rise when he reached the railhead. He haw'd the mules toward the ground where Maury had her washlines. She wouldn't be there at this hour, but her tent was undoubtedly near the lines . . . he caught sight of a campfire and headed for it.

Drawing rein outside the circle of firelight, he watched as a gangling young man tucked a fiddle under his chin and tested its tune.

There weren't many women in the group around the fire. Most of the brawny workmen had to pair with each other for the dance. But one man had a girl as his partner — and even in the shadowy firelight her hair was as wildly brilliant as fresh cut copper.

From the shadows he watched her dance, her skirts swirling and the coppery hair flagging out at each toss of her head. She smiled, laughed, exchanged words with the other dancers. And when the fiddler was done his tune, they all dropped to the ground, laughing breathlessly.

"Hullo there!" someone shouted. It was the man who'd been Maury's partner. He raised a hand, pointing in Dev's direction. "You! Skulking there in the dark, who are you?"

Dev stepped down from the wagon and walked into the circle of firelight.

"The buffalo skinner!" Maury called with a smile. "What brings you back to our camp by the dark of night?"

"Just driving past," he answered, feeling suddenly shy and very much out of place here.

The man with Maury got to his feet and stepped toward Dev, saying, "So you're the one my darling's been telling me about. Your name is Devereaux?"

Rising at his side, Maury said, "Buffalo skinner, it's my pleasure to introduce you to my own true love, the Fitzpatrick."

That brought a cheer from the track hands, and someone suggested, "Maybe the buffalo skinner'll join us in the dancing?"

"Yes." Maury grabbed at his hand, drawing him into the clearing. The men were rising again, to form a square, and the fiddler drew a warning chord with his bow. Then he launched into a tune and someone began the calls. At the shout of *Swing your partner,* Dev found Maury in his arms.

"What's the matter with you?" she asked, "Don't you fancy dancing? You've the natural grace of a half-ton boulder."

"It's been a long time since I danced with a white woman," he answered.

She laughed. "You've been stepping with the buffalo cows, I suppose?"

He tried to grin with her. But she was too close. He was too aware of the nearness of her body and the soft warmth of it. And there was the Fitzpatrick standing just outside the square, clapping to the music. *Her own true love,* she'd called him. As they stepped into a grand-right-and-left, he grabbed at one of the bystanders, hauling him into the set and dropping out. He wanted to get away — from the dancing and

83

from Maury. But as he started for his team a heavy hand fell onto his shoulder. Wheeling, he faced the Fitzpatrick.

"I'll have a word with you," the man said softly. He drew Dev into the shadows behind the wagon. "You're new here and it might be you're a bit ignorant as yet. I wouldn't like evil to come to you so there are things I'll tell you. There ain't a finer girl in the world than Maury O'Neil and if a man were to lay a hand to her or speak a wrong word to her, there ain't a man at End-of-Track who wouldn't be — well — concerned for her. Most of all me. Understand?"

"Yeah," Dev muttered, not thinking so much of the threat as of Maury's words. *Her own true love, the Fitzpatrick.* This was her man, her choice. And he was a railroader. That would be important to Maury. What the hell right did he, Devereaux, have to imagine himself in her world? None — at least as long as his name was on that damned list.

The hand moved off his shoulder and Fitzpatrick said heartily, "As long as we're understanding each other, you'll come along back to the dance."

"I've got things I have to attend to," Dev mumbled, pulling away from the man and turning to his wagon. Whatever it was the Fitzpatrick said then, he didn't hear it. Walking slowly, he led the team toward the rails.

There was a light showing through the shaded window of the major's waycar. He halted the mules and climbed to the door. His knock was answered by a muffled call, "Who in the name of — oh, come on in."

Major Nordstadt was seated at the little table with a sheath of papers spread out in front of him. The glow of the pivot lamp over the table deepened the lines of his scowl as he looked toward Dev. As if he'd just discovered something unexpected and not very pleasant, he said slowly, "Well, well, well . . . I surely didn't think I'd see you again, Devereaux."

"What's the matter?" Dev asked, puzzled.

"You, Devereaux, are a first prize liar with more brass than brains. To come back here now . . . you . . ." The major shook his head as if he were at a loss for words.

Completely taken aback, Dev found himself stammering, "I — I — what did I do?"

"You took me in completely with that story of yours. But no man plays me for a fool more than once. And if you had a hand in wrecking Mike Conner, I'll find proof of it and I'll hang you for it!"

"Major, I don't understand," Dev said

desperately. "What did I do?"

"Do you deny it? Some of our people were there in Laramie the night you got there. I got a full report of how you and one of Bannerman's hired killers set out to drain and raze the town together." Sarcastically, he added, "To kill the pain?"

Dev slumped back against the wall. He couldn't deny it. How the hell could he explain it? He said vaguely, "Danforth's dead."

The major's expression did not change. Cold voiced, he asked, "Did you kill him?"

"No!" Dev almost winced at the question, and the tone of it. "He was already dead when I got to Laramie. Dead and buried."

"I can check that easily enough."

He nodded. "A man name of Johnny Stark shot him in an argument of some kind."

The major frowned thoughtfully. "I'll listen to you one more time, Devereaux. You'd better have a good story."

He listened gravely and interrupted for details as Dev told him the whole of it — everything that had happened from the time he left End-of-Track up til his memories faded into drunken fragments — everything except the moments he could remember with Ruby Bannerman. And when he'd said it all, the major asked, "What do you intend to do now that Danforth is dead?"

"I've got to stick here and work until I get together a stake. Then I'll take out back-tracking Danforth."

"Why?"

Dev looked at him, surprised. It seemed obvious. "I've got nowhere else to look. Maybe I can find something — someone — on his back trail that'll give me an idea who he was working with at Willis Siding."

Something stirred behind the hanging blanket that divided the little waycar into two rooms. Noah Freedman stepped out and said, apologetically, "Gentlemen, I couldn't help but overhear the conversation. There's coffee made and I thought you might like some."

The major grinned. "You'll join us, won't you?" he asked as he cleared space on the table for cups.

Noah set out the coffee and when he had seated himself, the major asked, "What do you think about it?"

Noah spoke slowly, speculatively: "I think Corporal Devereaux may have brought us an interesting problem. This boy, Asa Engels, do you suppose he was trying to damage the track?"

"It's possible," Dev answered. "That story he gave me was about as far-fetched as . . .

well, as my side of what happened at Willis Siding. I guess that's why I went along with it. Right now I don't have much stomach for condemning a man on circumstantial evidence."

Noah nodded. "I wouldn't condemn the boy. I'd investigate. If there's a possibility he could lead us to the ones who wrecked Mike Conners. . . ."

"There'd be no harm in investigating," the major said. "Dev, you've met this boy and his family and they think well enough of you to sell you a horse on your promise. You'll be seeing them again. . . ."

"Yessir, but I think they'd have sold that poor old hack to anybody who'd give them half-a-promise. They strike me as a hard-shelled bunch that won't unbend easy to anybody."

"That may be so, but it's well worth trying. Our other lead is no better."

"What other lead?"

"Just camp gossip. Word's around that one of the businessmen from Laramie wants to keep the railhead camp in this area as long as possible. He's invested a lot of money and built permanently in the town. If he could put obstacles in the way of our finishing here and moving on, he'd profit by it."

"Dolph Bannerman?" Dev asked.

The major nodded. "Where was Bannerman when Mike was wrecked?"

"Jarrett told me he was off to Cheyenne on business."

"And where was Mike wrecked?"

"Between here and Cheyenne."

The major didn't comment.

"Hell, I don't know," Dev muttered. "That's pretty circumstantial evidence, too."

"Yes," the major said. "And I've got no stomach for condemning a man on it myself. But I intend to get at the truth about the wreckers, about the Engels boy, about Bannerman — and about you, Devereaux."

"You've met Engels and you're working for Bannerman," Noah said. "You're in a better position than anyone else around here to investigate them both."

The major added, "You'd be doing a very important job for us, Dev."

"Are you asking *me* to work for the railroad, Major?"

Sighing, he answered, "In my official position as a representative of shareholders, I couldn't rightfully ask you the time of day while your name's on that list. In my official position I should have reported you to General Jack. What I'm asking is personal. I need your help."

"Do you trust me?"

"I want to. You think I'd have busted a gut about your spree in Laramie if I didn't? Do you think I'd be asking your help at all if I didn't?" he extended a hand.

Dev accepted it.

VII

Dev left the railhead camp at dawn. He wanted to be well from it by the time the sun was full up. He wanted to be well away from any chance of running into Maury O'Neil.

The road to Laramie twisted through a wide ravine, overlooked by timbered ridges, where the early sun didn't reach. It was chilly there and the mules pulled at the bits, eager to move on. But Dev was in no hurry to be back in town. He sat with his elbows resting on his knees and his thoughts drifting from Maury O'Neil to the talk he'd had with the major. And back again to the red-haired girl. Something plucked suddenly at the sleeve of his short coat, and the crack of a rifle echoed between the ridges.

He threw himself down, out of the wagon, moving instinctively. As he dropped, one hand was looping the reins over the brake handle. The other grabbed for the Spencer. He caught it as another shot snapped out, lead grooving into the seat where he'd been.

He had the Spencer against his shoulder and was sighting along the barrel toward the ridge from which the shots had come. He saw nothing there to aim at, though.

The hidden rifle cracked again and this time he saw the hint of powder smoke. He could feel the slug brush past his head.

The mules were anxious, jerking the wagon fitfully, as he looked up from its cover, aiming. He triggered the rifle just as the ambusher fired again.

The near mule reared with a snorting scream and fell, its legs flailing.

Dev chambered another cartridge. Sure of his target now, he fired. There was no answering shot. He fired again, then waited. The strangled gasping and thrashing of the downed mule cut through the morning stillness. And there was another sound — hoofbeats fading into the distance.

Holding the Spencer at ready, he walked cautiously from behind the wagon. Nothing happened. There was no shot.

He went to the mule, lying on its side with a sharp sliver of rib bone thrust out through its hide. Blood oozed from the wound and trickled from its nostrils. It tried to lift up its head as he stepped in front of it. Setting the muzzle of the Spencer against the animal's broad forehead, he triggered it. The strained gasping for breath stopped.

Dev glanced back toward the ridge where the ambusher had been hidden. Then he turned to the standing mule and began stripping it of harness. When it was bared to the bridle, he shorted the reins with his knife and swung up onto its back.

Unaccustomed to a rider, the mule shied under him and humped. But as he slapped its rump with the rein ends, it broke into a frightened gallop, and he let it run. It responded to the bit and he turned it toward the ridge.

He found sign easily enough. A horse had stood tied while its rider went afoot up to the rocks, then returned again. The horse had been mounted — ridden away. Dev climbed back onto the mule and followed. The trail led across a backslope and into the woods. That was where he found the ambusher.

The horse was nibbling at the brush. The ambusher hung by one ankle from a stirrup, sprawling limply on the ground. As Dev approached, the horse looked up suspiciously, swinging its rump away from him, and the body moved, dragging like a half-full sack.

Dev stepped off the mule and walked up

slowly, careful not to spook the horse. He caught at the reins, then bent to look at the body. It was Asa Engels. He was very dead.

When Dev rode into the Engel's farmyard, it was with the Spencer over the mule's withers and his finger on the trigger. He halted at the edge of the woods and called out.

Wearily, Engels' wife stepped onto the porch. She wiped her hands on her apron and called back, "Who is it?"

He reined in toward her then, halting at the porch steps. Her eyes touched him with the vaguest of recognition and then went to the body over the saddle of the pony he led.

"Asa?" she said. There was no surprise, no emotion in her voice. It was as if she'd been expecting this moment.

"What is it, Maw?" The girl stepped out onto the porch. She gazed at Dev as she spoke.

"Your brother, Asa. He's dead," the woman said. She glanced at Dev. "He *is* dead, ain't he?"

"Yes, ma'am."

The girl looked at the body then. Her lupine eyes were bright with excitement. "Was it the railroaders or Bannerman?" she asked.

Dev looked from face to face. It was hard to understand. The mother seemed so casual, the sister without sorrow. Didn't they have any feeling for the boy? Was this initial shock? Or was it something they'd anticipated for so long that it was no shock at all?

"It was his Paw's doing," Mrs. Engels said. "As sure as if Jube done it himself, it was his doing."

"He tried to ambush me and I shot back. I hit him," Dev told her. "I didn't know who it was til I found him dead."

She nodded.

"Why'd he do it?" he asked.

The girl started to answer. "Paw'd never let him go along. He said Asa was too young so he . . ."

Mrs. Engels cut the girl short. "Mister," she said, her eyes on Dev seeming as though she were looking straight through him, "you'd better get before Jube and Lige come back or likely they'll kill you."

"Is there anything I can do? Can I take care of the body for you?"

She shook her head. "It was Paw's doing. Let him tend the boy. You get."

As she turned and walked back into the house, Dev dropped the horse's reins and heeled the mule around.

"Wait," the girl called. "They won't be back for a while. You could stay and visit a bit."

He looked at her, at the unnaturally bright lupine eyes and the color-flushed cheeks. She was smiling coyly. "My name's Rebecca. Folks call me Becky. You call me Becky."

"Your brother's dead," he said.

She shrugged as if it were none of her concern. "We could go for a walk and you could tell me about yourself." Leaning her head against a porch post, she touched her fingers lightly to her lips; ran them along her cheek and down her throat. "You got nice eyes," she said.

Was she half-witted, he wondered as he touched his hand to the brim of his hat. "Goodbye, Miss Becky."

She called after him, "You'll come back to see me again, won't you?"

He kicked the mule into a trot.

As he reached the crest of the ridge, he drew rein and looked out over the road. Something was raising dust in the distance. Shading his eyes, he made it out to be a wagon, and he started to meet it.

He was close when he recognized the driver — recognized her slim figure and the brilliant red hair that tumbled from under

95

the neck frill of her bonnet. He was too close to turn back. She'd already spotted him.

"You low, lying, sneaking black Firbolg!" she called in greeting. Drawing rein on the team, she stood up. "Oh, have you come to this now, astraddle a bony-backed, long-eared, flea-bitten mule?"

He reached up and pushed the hat back on his head as he came up alongside her wagon. "One of my team got hurt. I had to shoot him."

Her eyes widened and the scowl faded from her face. "Oh," she said in a very small voice.

"I'd like to borrow your team," he said. "I've got a cargo for Laramie and I don't want to leave it on the road. If I could borrow that span of yours, and haul my wagon in, I'd come back later for yours."

She considered a moment, then picked up her lines. "Well now, come along. Let's see what's to be done."

Dev trotted ahead to his rig and looked down at the carcass of the dead mule. The flies had already begun to swarm over its bloody side. It was an ugly thing for the girl to see.

She halted her wagon behind his and stood up, waiting. Finally she called out to him, "Aren't you even enough of a gentleman to help a girl down from her buggy?"

Reluctantly, he dropped off the mule and held out a hand to her. Why did it have to be Maury who came along just at this time? Her slim fingers wrapped around his hand and she held out the other hand to him. When he accepted it, she started to step down. But as she stepped she leaned forward, almost falling. And she was in his arms.

He felt her body against his and saw her face upturned toward him, her lips barely parted. He kissed her. And he felt her yield, accept, return the kiss.

For a long moment he held her mouth with his. And when he looked into her face again, her eyes were closed, her lips still slightly parted.

He took a step back, stammering, "I — I'm sorry." And immediately he felt that it was the most foolish, useless thing he could have said.

"Are you now?" She opened her eyes and her voice was softly husky. "You're a strange, dark man in more ways than just your features, Mister Devereaux. Is it in you to speak your mind or will you run away from me again as you did last night?"

He gestured vaguely, then snapped out

the words, "If I ran away from you it's because I've got good reason."

She started to say something else, then hesitated. Finally, she said, "I'll ask you no more, for it's yours to tell me or not, as you wish. But I'll tell you it's an evil thing to brood over dark thoughts alone." She turned her face away from him then, and he busied himself with the team.

When he drew the wagon up in front of the freight office two men came through the door toward him. One was the agent, the other Hal Jarrett.

Jarrett's face was uncommonly grave as he glanced from Dev to the girl beside him, then to the team and the mule tied at the tailgate. "I've been waiting for you," he said. "You got a long story?"

"I've got a dead mule and Miss O'Neil's rig is off the road back a ways. She lent me her team," he answered. He didn't want to mention the ambush or the death of Asa Engels in front of Maury. "Is there somebody here who can take a pair of horses to fetch her wagon while I drive her on where she's going?"

"I'll send somebody for the wagon," Jarrett answered. "Right now *you* had better get over and see Ruby Bannerman. She's had me waiting here for you all day."

"Right now I . . ."

"Right now you go see Ruby," Jarrett said firmly.

Looking into his face, Dev decided that whatever was wrong must be serious. He asked, "Hal, will you look out for Miss O'Neil till I get back?"

Jarrett pulled off his hat as he spoke to Maury: "It'd be my pleasure, Miss O'Neil."

As Dev dropped down off the seat, he muttered, "Take good care of her, Hal. Or you'll answer to me."

He hurried through the crowd in the *Palace* and up to the office. Ruby was standing by the window, gazing out. When she turned to face him, her eyes were hard. "Where've you been?"

"I took a load of freight to Gil Nash's," he told her. "And I brought a load back."

"Who told you to do that?"

Why was she so angry, he wondered. "It's the job you hired me for. Isn't it?"

"Damnit, Devereaux . . ." she started, then stopped. She took a step toward him and when she spoke again, her voice was quietly tense. "Who is that girl?"

"What girl?"

"That redheaded creature who came in with you. Is she something you picked up at

Nash's?"

"She . . ."

"Don't deny it," her words cut harshly across his. "The Breed saw you. And so did I."

"I'm not denying a damned thing," he snapped back. "I got ambushed out there and killed a man — a boy. One of my mules was killed. When Miss O'Neil came along, I borrowed her team to bring in your freight."

She turned back to the window and looked out, though she seemed to be looking at nothing in particular. "You were gone three nights," she said, her back to him.

"It takes that long to drive out and back."

She looked at him again, her lips framing words that she didn't speak. She started toward him, the window haloing her hair, the spill of sunlight outlining her ivory cheek. "Devereaux," she said very softly. Her tongue darted over her lips, moistening them, leaving them slightly parted.

She took another step and she was very close. Her eyes were hot green flame. Putting her hands on his shoulders, she moved them slowly, caressingly, around his neck. Again she said, "Devereaux."

His own hands were on her waist, feeling the warmth of her body through her clothing. He jerked them away, stepping back and pulling her arms from around his neck.

"Is *that* what you hired me for?" he snapped.

She wheeled, tossing her head, and she turned to him again, the crystal green eyes were narrowed with anger. "Yes!" she spat. "Now get out!"

He slammed the door behind him.

As he shoved through the crowd in the saloon, headed for the door, he felt a hand touch his arm. The fingers gripped to halt him.

"Devereaux."

He turned to face Dolph Bannerman.

"Ruby's been waiting to see you," Bannerman said. His voice was mild and restrained as if there were things he wanted to say, but never would.

"I've seen her already," Dev muttered.

"So quickly? What's the matter? Have you two been arguing or something?"

"Kinda." He shifted weight nervously. He wanted to get away from Bannerman. He wanted to get out of the saloon, into the fresh air and sunlight. And he wanted to get back to Maury O'Neil. But the hand on his arm was firm.

"Come on, sit down. Have a drink with me," Bannerman said gently. Despite the pleasant tone, it was an order.

"Thanks, but no."

"I want to talk to you," he insisted.

"Why? I'm busted off this job, ain't I? What's there to talk about?"

"Hold on. You owe me too much money to quit on me like this. Sit down and talk with me, will you?"

That was true, Dev thought. He owed Bannerman a debt of hard cash for the things he'd bought at the mercantile. Whether he wanted it or not, he had an obligation to the man. He let himself be steered through the crowd to a back table where a trio of teamsters sat. The men touched their hats to Bannerman and moved away without protest.

When they were seated and Bannerman had called for drinks, he drew a pair of cigars out of his pocket and offered Dev one.

"No thanks."

With a shrug he pocketed one and then lit the other. He held it in his hand, seeming to stare at it as he spoke. "Devereaux, anything Ruby wants, she gets. You understand that? *Anything.*" He did not look up.

The waiter set glasses in front of them, poured from the bottle, set it on the table and left. Bannerman didn't speak again until he was well out of earshot. Then he said, "You came into Laramie on a blind horse with nothing but holes in your pockets. Now you've got clothes, a gun, food in your belly and, if you want hard money, I'll give you an advance. Come the season, I'm willing to outfit you to go onto the buffalo range and hunt your fortune. You've probably never been so well off in your life as you are in the hire of the Bannermans. Don't ruin it for yourself by playing the fool."

Dev emptied his glass. Over the rim of it, he studied Bannerman, trying to understand him. But the face was expressionless, the eyes were veiled.

"Ruby's a forgiving woman," Bannerman was saying. "She's sensitive and easily hurt, but she's understanding." He reached into a pocket and pulled out a slip of paper and a pencil. With a quick sweep of his hand, he scrawled a few words on the paper and shoved it across the table toward Dev. "This is a note of credit any merchant in town will accept. You pick up a present for Ruby. Something nice. She'll . . . she'll . . ." The words seemed to catch in his throat. Without a look toward Dev, he got to his feet and stalked into the crowd.

Dev picked up the paper, starting to crumple it in his hand. He stopped and scanned it. He stared at the sweeping unadorned sprawl of Bannerman's handwriting, then looked up into the crowd. Bannerman was gone. He turned his eyes to the note again. The handwriting was very much like his own — the quick, ornamentless scribble a telegrapher develops transcribing the staccato of incoming code.

He folded the note carefully and stuffed it into his pocket. Slowly, he walked out of the saloon.

VIII

When Dev got back to the freightyards, Maury O'Neil was gone. So was Hal Jarrett.

All the freight agent could tell him was that the two had left together afoot, heading for the main street. He strode along the walk, looking through windows and asking loafers and finally he found one who could tell him that he'd seen Jarrett bringing a hired rig out of the livery stable. "Mebbe he took her for a drive," the man suggested with a wink. "You know Hal."

Dev was afraid that he did know Hal — at least that well. He cursed himself for having wasted so much time already as he hurried for the corral behind Bannerman's saloon.

It was coming dark.

He helped himself to a saddle and rode out at a gallop. Maury had told him she was going to visit friends named Sullivan who'd staked north of town. Chances were Jarrett had offered to drive her on to their place, he decided. At least Hal would have started in that direction. . . .

There was no chance of reading sign in the mixed prints on the road, especially not in the twilight. But he kept his eyes to the shoulders, looking for traces of a buggy turning off, until it was too dark to look any longer.

The moon rose shrouded with haze. It was well up when he reached the Sullivan farm. As he drew into the yard, a dog began to bark and in a moment light appeared in one window. The door was opened by a stocky man with a coat pulled over his night shirt. He held a lamp in one hand, and in the other a rifle at ready. Frowning toward Dev, he called, "Who is it? What's the matter?"

"I'm looking for Maury O'Neil! Is she here?"

"Should she be? Who are you to be asking after her at this hour?" the man asked.

"Have you seen her?" Dev insisted. "Is she here?"

"No," the man responded to the urgency

in Dev's voice. "What's the matter? Is there trouble at the railhead?"

Without answering, Dev wheeled the mare and rammed his heels into her heaving sides. With a snort of protest, she leaped into a gallop.

It was late — damned late — when he dropped out of the saddle in front of Bannerman's *Palace.* Striding in, he demanded of the bartender, "Have you seen anything of Hal Jarrett?"

The man jerked a thumb toward the stairs.

"Was there a — was anyone with him?"

The bartender shrugged and turned away.

Dev took the stairs two at a time. As he reached the top he saw the knife-thin edge of light under Jarrett's closed door. He headed toward it, then hesitated with his hand on the knob.

"Hal?" he called. He got a muffled grunt for an answer. Turning the knob, he shoved the door open. Jarrett was there — alone. He lay sprawled on his belly across the bed, his face buried in a pillow.

"Where's Maury O'Neil?" Dev demanded.

"Leave me be," Jarrett muttered without moving. He lay as limp as if he'd fallen.

"Where's Maury O'Neil?" Dev repeated.

Jarrett grunted. When he spoke, his voice was hoarse and muffled by the pillow. "At

Sullivan's. Leave me alone. I'm sick."

Dev reached out, digging his fingers into Jarrett's shoulder, jerking at it. Jarrett started for the gun he wore, but Dev's grip on his upper arm held him from it. "Jarrett!"

Dev's fisted right hand hovered over his face as Jarrett looked up. Three long gashes caked with dried blood striped the man's cheek. His lower lip was swollen, the skin broken where small sharp teeth had dug into it. Thickly, he said, "What's the matter?"

Dev opened his fist, slammed his palm hard across Jarrett's face. "You'd better tell me just what's happened."

"She's a wildcat, ain't she?" Jarrett tried to grin and winced. He flicked his tongue over his swollen lip. "She didn't exactly agree with me so I drove her on to Sullivan's. Why?"

Dev spoke slowly, fighting the anger in him. "She never got to Sullivan's."

"Oh."

"You want to tell me the *truth* now?"

Jarrett blinked. "Leggo my arm," he muttered.

Dev eased his fingers, but he didn't let go.

Jarrett looked at him with a hound dog expression and said mournfully, "I was just trying to be friendly. But she come at me all fangs and claws. I — I — hell, next thing I knew I was on my tail on the ground and she was slapping up the horse. She left me there afoot. I don't know where she went from there. I had to shank it back to town. I didn't even see her again. I hope to hell I never do — all the way back to town in them boots. I had to shank it."

"You better hope you *do* see her again," Dev snapped. He let go Jarrett's arm and stepped back. Jarrett let his head sink wearily into the pillow.

"Get up," Dev said.

"I can't. I'm sick."

"Come on, Hal. We've got to find that girl. You've got to show me where you left her."

"Where *she* left *me,*" Jarrett mumbled. Slowly he sat up and pressed his face into his hands. He looked at Dev over the tips of his fingers. "You're plumb determined, ain't you?"

"We've got to find her."

"I don't reckon I can blame you," Jarrett muttered. "Though I got a strong notion that one can take care of herself." Taking a tentative step, he winced. He mumbled through clenched teeth as he tipped the pitcher over the basin, then splashed water into his face. With a sigh, he turned to Dev and said, "All right I'll go."

"Well, come on, damnit," Dev snapped.

"Don't push me, friend," Jarrett said. "Hold on while I find my moccasins. I couldn't get them Texas boots on again with a prybar right now." He found them and pulled them on. Starting lamely toward the door, he muttered, "I done wrong and I'm sorry for it. But don't you never hit me openhanded again, friend."

They followed the Laramie road almost to the cut-off that led to Sullivan's before Jarrett turned into the grass. He led the way across a level toward a stand of aspen. Circling the trees, he drew rein. "It was about here we stopped the buggy," he said. "I told her it was a shortcut."

Dev swung off the pony and gathered a handful of twigs. Twisting them into a torch, he knelt to examine the ground. The grass was patchy and the earth damp enough to hold tracks. He could pick out where the horse had been halted. It had stood, then shied and bolted.

Jarrett listened curiously as Dev spoke what he saw in the prints. Then he said, "That's when she thrun me out'n the buggy. The pony jumped like a jackrabbit and off he went with her reining his rump and hollering. Maybe she busted a wheel."

"Come on," Dev grunted, following her trail. It went downslope, over the rock strewn field. The torch in his hand burned down and he started to twist another. Suddenly he froze, his hand outstretched. He frowned, listening. Yes, he heard it again. It was a faint murmur.

The wind scudded clouds across the moon, shadowing the rocky field. Then they passed and light washed down. In it, he saw a shadow moving among the shadows. It fluttered like a flag in the wind. Running toward it, he saw the girl. She lay among the rocks, her face toward the sky and the full skirts billowing around her. He dropped to his knees at her side, seeing the paleness of her face in the moonlight, and the dark stain that smeared over the front of her blouse.

He touched his fingertips to the blood-stained cloth. Under it, he could feel warmth and the slightest of movement. Incredulously he muttered, "She's been shot!"

Jarrett dropped off his horse and limped over. He bent to look at her as Dev put a hand to her forehead. She moaned and stirred. Her eyes fluttered open, looked up at Jarrett, and she screamed.

Dev moved. Without thought or plan he

swung. His fist rammed into Jarrett's face, sprawling him in the grass. Dev rose, his fists clenched, but Jarrett lay still.

Bending back to the girl, Dev saw that her eyes were closed again, and her breathing was shallow. He touched her shoulder, then straightened. There wasn't anything he could do for her here and now. The bleeding had stopped, but if he tried to move her on horseback, it might start up again. He had to get a wagon and medicines. He glanced around. Sullivan's place should be just a ways over the ridge. As he turned toward the horses, he almost stumbled over Hal Jarrett.

For a moment he paused, looking down at the unconscious man. Was Jarrett responsible for what had happened? Maybe he had left her out here alone but surely he hadn't actually shot her — had he? It didn't seem possible that Hal could shoot down a woman. But then it didn't seem possible that any man could have shot down Maury O'Neil. And just how well did he know Hal, he asked himself. The blank boyishness of Jarrett's face and the idiot grin were a mask — he'd admitted as much. But a mask for what?

He decided that he couldn't take a chance. Holding Jarrett's wrists, he dragged the limp body toward the nearest tree and propped him against it. He used strings from Jarrett's saddle to tie his hands behind the tree trunk. Then he stepped onto the calico, gathered the reins of Jarrett's geld, and headed for the Sullivan place.

As he came into the yard, the dog raised voice and in a moment the door swung open. Sullivan peered out, holding up his lamp. "You again?" he shouted. "God-damnit, man, what's going on?"

Dev told him in quick sparse words and in a few minutes the man had sent his son for the doctor and was in his wagon with his wife at his side, following Dev back. Mrs. Sullivan was out of the wagon the instant he drew rein. She set her husband to hold the light and ordered Dev to stay at a respectable distance while she spread back the blouse and examined the wound.

He paced impatiently while she worked. It seemed like a damned long time before she called him over and, wrapping Maury in quilts, they lifted her into the wagon.

"It's a terrible thing," Sullivan muttered. "Who could have done it?"

Then Dev remembered Jarret. He looked toward the tree and saw that he was conscious now and watching them through half-closed eyes. Unsheathing his knife, Dev slashed the thongs that held his wrists.

"Hell of a friend you are," Jarrett mumbled thickly as he rubbed at his arms. "I think you busted my jaw."

"Get in the wagon," Dev ordered.

Sullivan peered at Jarrett, his forehead wrinkling in a frown. "Is this the one that shot Maury?"

Dev hesitated. "I don't know."

"Thanks," Jarrett grunted. "Thanks a lot, old friend." He glanced around. "What have you done with my horse?"

"It's at Sullivan's. Get in the wagon."

Jarrett limped toward the wagon, mumbling under his breath. As he hoisted himself over the wall, he asked Mrs. Sullivan, "How is she?"

"Hurt bad," she snapped at him. Then she added more gently, "There's no bleeding and she's breathing easy."

Dev tied his mare to the tailgate and climbed into the wagon. Then Sullivan urged his horse on, taking the wagon over the rough ground as gently as he could. They had to go slowly and the crawling pace was almost unendurable. Dev looked down at Maury's pale face. She was still unconscious. Was it possible that Jarrett had done this, he asked himself again, glancing toward the gunman.

Jarrett had curled up in a corner of the wagon, resting his head on one arm. His breathing was deep and regular, and Dev wondered how the hell he could sleep at a time like this. Either his conscience was clear — or maybe he didn't have one.

Moonlight glinted on brass at Jarrett's thigh and Dev realized suddenly that he hadn't thought to disarm him. Moving with slow caution, he reached for the butt of the Colt. Suddenly the holster was empty — the gun was in Jarrett's hand and leveled toward Dev.

Raising his half-open hands, Dev judged the distance between his knuckles and Jarrett's face. It was too far.

Jarrett's grin was lopsided. He raised himself up on his elbow. "You shoulda thought of that while you had my hands tied."

"Next time I will," Dev muttered.

"There won't be a next time," Jarrett said. "You got a hard fist, but when it comes to guns you're out'n your class, friend. You start any more games like this one and I'll save myself a sore jaw by putting a ball through your gut first thing."

Dev was aware of Sullivan bending slightly, trying to reach under the bench for his rifle. Jarrett didn't even glance at the man, as he said, "I'm tired and I'm hungry and I ache, Mister Sullivan. And I ain't in a very pleasant mood. I'd thank you not to give me no trouble. That horse ought to have all your attention."

As Sullivan's back straightened and he took the reins in both hands, Jarrett spoke to Dev again. "You know, old friend, you're loco. Pure crazy. The way you've been carrying on tonight . . . maybe it's that girl there that's addled your wits and if it is I reckon I can't rightly hold you responsible. If any man in his right mind was to try pushing me around the way you been doing, I'da killed him long since. But I got a notion I want to see just what kind of hell you're gonna stir up next." He slipped the Colt back into its holster and put his head down on his arm again. As he closed his eyes he added, "Just you keep your hands away from my sidearm. Riles me something awful a man lays a hand to my gun."

"Damn you, Jarrett," Dev said. "You don't make sense."

"Am I supposed to?"

"Either you're telling me the truth about Maury O'Neil or else you're the slipperiest slick-tongued liar this side of the river."

"I'm both, old friend," Jarrett said with a yawn. "Now, leave me sleep, will you?"

Dev leaned back against the wall of the wagon. Maybe Jarrett was telling the truth, he thought. He'd had a notion that maybe in a fit of prideful temper Jarrett had fired at the girl when she'd refused his advances. Maybe that wasn't the way it had happened at all. But if it wasn't Jarrett, then who — why?

Nothing seemed to make sense.

IX

The doctor arrived in a phaeton drawn by a shaggy, hammer-headed mountain pony. He strode into the house, a big, bony-faced man wrapped in a great coat. He peeled it off and rubbed his hands together, flexing the fingers, as he glanced from the girl in the bed to Hal Jarrett.

"I'm Doctor Bloch," he said. "Which one is my patient?"

Solemnly, Jarrett nodded toward the girl. "She's been shot."

"By whom?" Bloch asked as he began his examination.

"We don't know — yet," Sullivan answered.

"When you find out, send for me," the doctor told them. "I've got a handsome length of hemp that needs stretching. Mrs.

Sullivan, is there any hot water?"

Sullivan fetched the kettle and the doctor washed his hands. Then he called for fresh water in the basin. "And give some to him, too," he added, jerking his head toward Jarrett.

"Huh?" Hal grunted.

"Wash your face," the doctor told him. "And if anything else hurts, wash it, too. I'll look at you when I'm through with the girl."

"I hurt all over," Jarrett muttered. "Mostly my feet."

The doctor had turned his attention to Maury. He didn't look up as he asked, "What happened to your feet?"

"Long walk in tight boots."

"Why don't you soak them?"

Jarrett grinned. "Hell, I never thought of that. Mrs. Sullivan, you reckon I could borrow a bucket full of that water?"

"Help yourself," she answered. She watched him curiously as he set up the bucket and then eased his feet into the water, grimacing and then sighing.

"It's a clean wound," Bloch said suddenly. "The worst part is the blood she's lost. She's weak but she's young and hearty."

"Is she conscious?" Dev asked.

"She's asleep. Exhausted."

"Can I speak to her?"

"No," the doctor snapped. "Let her sleep til she wakes of her own accord."

"I've got to ask her what happened," Dev told him.

"It's kinda important," Jarrett added.

"You'll get your answer in time," the doctor said. "Right now she needs rest more than revenge." He turned to Jarrett: "Now you."

Jarrett squirmed, grunted and muttered as the doctor swabbed at the cuts on his face. He was still muttering when Bloch snapped his bag closed and shrugged on his coat.

"She'll be all right," Bloch told them with a nod toward Maury. "Now the rest of you get some sleep. All of you."

"I'm agreeable to that," Jarrett said.

Sullivan glanced from his face to Dev's. "You fellers can sleep in the barn."

There was a thin drizzle of rain coming down when Dev and Jarrett headed out. But the small barn was snug against the damp winds. A sad-eyed hound met them and sniffed at their feet as they spread the quilts Mrs. Sullivan had loaned them and when Dev had put out the lantern and sprawled out, the dog lay down beside him, resting its big head on his chest.

He lay there, his eyes open to the darkness, listening to the rain and scratching at the dog's neck. The way it had begun to come down, it would be washing out any tracks. He wondered if Maury had seen anything or if she'd been shot from ambush. And over and over he asked himself why anyone would have wanted to shoot her? He pushed the hound's head off his chest, shifting his position and trying to ease the weary ache of his muscles.

"Ain't you asleep yet?"

The sound of Jarrett's voice startled him. He answered, "No."

"That redheaded gal's really got you addled, ain't she?"

"Shows that bad?"

"After the way you run out on Ruby? Hell, you'd have to be loco," Hal said. "The surest way to addle a man is to get him involved with a good-looking woman, like that gal."

"All Ruby wanted was a stud horse," Dev grunted.

"You finally figured that out, did you?"

"I figured out that much, but that's about all," he admitted.

"You ain't as smart as I thought," Jarrett said. "Ruby sure was riled about you taking that wagon to Nash's the way you did. She was madder'n hell at me for letting you go. But I tell you, friend, I never figured you'd be that dumb. And I didn't have no notion that agent'd be damnfool enough to give you a trip without Ruby's say-so."

"He wasn't going to but Stark come along and talked him into it."

"Johnny Stark? I'll be damned." He sounded amused. "I reckon that makes it all clear."

"Not to me, it don't. Maybe you'd like to explain it all for me," Dev said. He waited, but Hal didn't answer. In the darkness, though, he could hear him moving. He reached for the lamp and lit it. The sudden glow showed him Jarrett sitting up and frowning thoughtfully.

"Maybe," Jarrett drawled, as if he were talking to himself. "Now that Johnny's messed things up between you and Ruby he *might* lay off, but it ain't likely. He don't like no loose ends."

"Lay off?"

He nodded and looked at Devereaux, studying him. "You stand a good chance of getting yourself killed, you know. Maybe you got a right to know why."

Dev waited. He realized that Jarrett was arguing something with himself and if he was going to explain he'd do it in his own time.

"I got tied up with Bannerman back in

Julesburg," Hal said slowly, gazing into space. "Back then it was Danforth who was Ruby's special friend. When she started to get friendly with me and Dolph encouraged it, I got right curious so one night I got Danforth likkered up and pried enough out of him to put together the story.

"Ruby and Dolph were married back before the war. You know for yourself she's a whole lot of woman and I reckon he must have been quite a man. He and Danforth run goods through the blockade during the war. And she went right along with them, living off the land and running from the troops and fighting back when they had to. All through it, she stuck right at Dolph's side. Then he got shot up. Hurt bad." He hesitated as if it were hard for him to go on with the story. "Hurt permanent. And Ruby being the kind of woman she is, she needed — like you said — she needed a stud horse. But Dolph wasn't one anymore. So she went to Danforth, and maybe others too, I don't know. When I come along she liked my looks. After me it was Johnny Stark and then you. . . ."

"And Bannerman *encourages* it? Doesn't he *care*?" Dev asked.

"Of course he cares," Jarrett snapped back at him. "You don't understand, do you? He *loves* her. And she loves him. You and me and fellers like us, we hell around and think we know all about love but we don't — not none of us. Not the way it is between those two. He gives her everything — if there's anything she wants, he'll get it for her. And what he can't give her himself, he sees to it she gets, no matter what it is.

"Of course he don't like it none. But what else can he do? So she picks out a man she likes the looks of and Dolph gets him for her — like a stud horse." He leaned back, resting his head on his hands, looking at nothing. After a moment, he started talking again. "That's what Johnny Stark don't understand. He don't know he's just a stud horse to her. He's got a notion she's really fond of him and he thinks he could take her away from Dolph — and all Dolph's property, too. That's why he killed Danforth and that's why he'll kill you."

"I don't get it," Dev said.

"Stark was afraid Ruby might still have some feelings for Danforth, so first good chance he got he forced Charlie into a draw and killed him. Then you come along and she decided she wanted you. That shook Johnny up pretty bad, but he couldn't kill you outright then and there. Not while Ruby favored you. He's afraid it would turn her against him, same as he's afraid to kill Dolph outright. So he pulled that stunt with the freight agent and got you out of town for a few days. Looks like it worked — it busted you and Ruby up, all right."

"What about you?" Dev asked. "You said you were friendly with her. Has Stark got his gun cocked for you, too?"

"Kinda," Jarrett admitted. "But he ain't particularly worried about me. He figures I'm too much of a fool to be any threat to him and his plans. And he's a mite afraid I got a faster gun hand, too."

Dev's thoughts went back to Danforth. He asked, "Was Charlie any good with a gun?"

"Not much. He wasn't a hired man. He was a partner. Him and Dolph had been partners since back during the war. Dolph was the brains, though. Charlie wasn't much of anything except a dandy. If he hadn't been such a dandy, always sniffing around and making up to Ruby, Stark might not have killed him. If you stay away from her he *might* not kill you."

"I don't give a hoot in hell about Ruby Bannerman," Dev said. "I don't want anything to do with her."

Jarrett reached for the lantern and killed the flame. "You just make that real clear to

123

Johnny," he muttered.

Dev lay back, gazing into the darkness, and going over the things Hal had said. There was a lot to be thought out.

There was wind up high. It feathered the hanging edges of the mass of cloud that stretched from horizon to horizon. Dev leaned a shoulder against the barn door frame and looked at the cold, dull drizzle. It was the kind of rain that seemed to seep into everything, even a person's bones.

"Dev?"

He wheeled and looked at Jarrett.

"Is she awake yet?" Jarrett asked. He still lay in his quilts and held one arm over his face as if he had to shield his eyes against the thin gray light of morning.

"I don't know," Dev answered.

Looking past him Jarrett asked, "Miserable day?"

He nodded. "If there were any tracks, they'll be washed out by now."

"Maybe she saw something," Jarrett suggested as he crawled out of the quilts. "Maybe she'll remember."

Glancing back at the sky, Dev started to button his coat. He wheeled back as he felt Jarrett's hand fall heavily on his shoulder.

Jarrett's other hand shot out, slamming

into his face. It was sudden and unexpected. He had no chance to duck it or roll with the blow. It rocked his head back, sending a shock of pain through his face. Braced against the wall, he shook his head. Through hazed eyes, he could see Jarrett stood poised, waiting.

"I owed you that, maybe more," Hal said. "You want to call it even?"

Dev rubbed the back of his hand across his mouth. He said, "Who shot Maury O'Neil!"

Angrily, Jarrett turned away. He busied himself with making a fuss over the hound and then followed wordlessly as Dev headed for the house.

The kitchen was warm. There was a bright twinkling of flame behind the firedoor of the big iron stove and a rich scent of burning wood and baking biscuits filled the room.

"Don't just stand there like a pair of drowned pigs," Mrs. Sullivan greeted them. "Come on in and have some breakfast."

"How's Miss O'Neil?" Dev asked as he pulled off his coat.

"Still asleep, but she should be wakening soon. Rosy, my oldest girl is with her. She'll call us when she wakens." Mrs. Sullivan set cups on the table and tilted the big coffee pot over them. Then she started slicing bacon into a pan on the stove. She'd got the meat cooking and was setting out eggs when the bedroom door opened.

The girl who looked out called, "Maw, I think she's gonna wake up."

The four of them crowded in and surrounded the bed, watching as Maury tossed her head restlessly. Her eyelids fluttered and opened.

"Maury," Dev said, his voice little more than a whisper.

She looked at him. He could see her eyes focus and then she smiled. "Oh, thank God it's you," she murmured. Then she saw Mrs. Sullivan and asked, "What's happened?"

"Hush, child." She put a hand to Maury's forehead. "It's all right now, you're in my house."

"Do you remember what happened?" Dev asked.

"What happened?" she repeated after him. She frowned then glanced around. Her eyes went to Hal Jarrett, standing at the foot of the bed. "You!"

Intensely, Dev asked, "Was it him?"

She didn't seem to understand.

"Tell him," Jarrett said. "Tell him, was it me?"

She frowned as she gazed at him. "You?"

Her voice was vague and there was confusion in her eyes.

"You *do* remember, don't you?" Jarrett asked.

Slowly, she nodded. "Yes. You did look so funny sitting there in the bushes when you fell out of the wagon. But I was too mad then to laugh. I'd have scratched your eyes out." She turned to Dev. "You've black, evil friends, you know."

"Do you remember what happened after you thrun me out'n the buggy?" Jarrett asked her. "Do you remember being shot at?"

"He rose up out of the rocks," she said softly, "with nothing on but his britches. He had a rifle to his shoulder and he scared the horse, rising up like that, so sudden and silent. The horse went up on his hind legs and I saw the rifle flash. A red Indian, he was, with his hair down on his shoulders and great white marks on his chest."

"An Indian," Jarrett repeated. "You hear that, Dev? An Indian."

Dev nodded, but it didn't add up.

"Now, you've heard what you wanted to hear," Mrs. Sullivan was saying. "You go back to the kitchen and if you're hungry, help yourselves to breakfast while I tend to the girl here." She waved her hands at them as if she were shooing chickens.

Jarrett headed for the stove. He cut a dab of butter and dropped it into the skillet. Then he cracked an egg over it. Glancing at Dev, he asked, "What's the matter now? Your girl's awake and she told you what you wanted to know. She's gonna be all right and it ain't me that shot her. And here's breakfast almost ready. But you sure don't look very happy about it."

"She said it was an Indian," Dev muttered.

Jarrett cracked another egg. "That's what you ain't happy about? You sorry it wasn't me that done it?"

"It doesn't sound right to me."

"It was an Indian," he said firmly. "Is there any reason she'd lie about it? It was one of them Sioux and I got a notion where we could look for them. If we got a few fellers together — fellers like that doctor — and rode out we could find 'em. Show 'em how we feel about having our women shot at."

"I can't believe it was the Lakota," Dev told him. "Not the way it happened. That ain't their way of doing things."

The eggs had begun to scorch. Jarrett jerked the pan off the fire, then sucked at his fingertips. He looked at Dev and asked, "Why? Hell, they got no respect for a white

128

woman."

"Sure, they'd as soon kill a woman as a man, but they take women's scalps too. This one, though — after he shot her, he just left her. Handsome red hair like that and he didn't even touch it," Dev said.

Jarrett had piled a plate with eggs and bacon. He set it on the table, then loaded another plate and handed it to Dev. "Maybe he wanted the horse worse than he wanted the hair," he suggested. "Likely it started to run away and he went after it."

"Maybe," Dev muttered doubtfully. He sipped at his coffee, then tasted the eggs. "You're not a very good cook."

"It ain't my regular trade. If you don't like my cooking, you can feed yourself."

"Don't apologize."

Jarrett forked a cut of egg into his mouth. Frowning critically, he chewed, swallowed, and announced, "I've ate worse."

"Did you do the cooking that time too?"

"Time I'm thinking of was . . . what's the matter?"

Dev had waved a hand to quiet him. "Horses coming. Two of them."

He cocked his head. "You got a good ear. I don't hear a thing but . . . yeah, now I hear 'em."

The dog began yapping as the horses

came into the yard. Dev looked out as Sullivan swung down off his saddle horse. The dog was trotting around, sniffing at the pony he'd led in. It was a sorrel mare with buggy harness still on its back.

"Good morning," Sullivan called as he saw Dev. "Will you look what I've found in the woods?"

"Hey, that's the horse I hired yesterday," Jarrett said as he looked over Dev's shoulder. "Where'd you get her? Where's the buggy? I still owe the stable for the hire of it."

Sullivan stepped into the kitchen and stripped off his hat and slicker. "In the woods," he repeated as he poured himself a cup of coffee. "I found her there with the wreck of the buggy dragging behind her, the wheels all busted. It's a wonder she hadn't thrown herself. But no, there she stood eating away at the bushes just as calm as you please."

"An Indian," Dev said sarcastically. He looked at Jarrett. "An Indian that wanted the horse more than he wanted a bright red scalplock."

Jarrett was frowning. He wheeled away from Dev, muttering firmly, "An Indian."

Sullivan had gulped at his coffee and was prodding the scraps of egg left in the frypan. "What happened to the food? It don't look so good. Where's my Missus?"

"Right here," Mrs. Sullivan answered as she came through the bedroom door. "Hold your horses. You'll get your breakfast in good time. I've been changing a dressing."

"I'm a hungry man," Sullivan mumbled.

His wife turned to Dev. "Maury's asked to see you." She led him into the bedroom.

Maury was propped up on pillows, with a shawl around her shoulders and her hair in thick braids. There was color in her face again, and she smiled at him. "I've a favor to ask of you, Mister Devereaux. Would you ride back to End-of-Track for me and carry word of what's happened to the Fitz-patrick?"

He looked into her golden eyes. It wasn't an errand he fancied. But he nodded.

"You must tell him I'm well and he shouldn't be worried." As she looked at him her smile faded. She asked, "What's the matter?"

"Nothing," he mumbled. "I'd better be going."

"Wait," she called as he started to turn. "You're thinking dark thoughts, aren't you?"

"No."

"Is it because of what happened? Because I got shot?"

"No," he repeated.

Her eyes serious, she asked, "You'll come back, won't you?"

He nodded. Quickly, he stepped through the door and closed it behind him. In the kitchen he spoke to Jarrett. "Come on, we're going to the railhead."

"Not me," Hal said emphatically. He ran a hand along the welts on his face. "Word travels fast and them fellers at the railhead are a randy bunch of bullies. They ain't no friends of mine to begin with. I got no notion to ride into the middle of them marked like this."

"Afraid?" Dev asked him.

He looked indignant. "One at a time — or two or three at once — fist or guns, I'll take on them railroaders. But not the whole damned camp at once."

Dev shrugged on his surcoat and headed out of the kitchen with Jarrett following after, still talking. "You know how it is. That there girl, she ain't the kind . . . well. Folks don't take too well to . . . hell, you know what I mean, Dev."

Their horses were tied in the barn. Dev pulled the mare's nose out of a manger and forced the bridle on her.

"If you've got any sense," Jarrett was saying, "you'll stay away from that camp too.

At least for a while. You're mixed up in this, you know. You ain't gonna have an easy time explaining it to them rowdies yourself."

"Maybe that's so," Dev grunted as he heaved the saddle onto his pony's back. "But Miss O'Neil wants me to take word to the Fitzpatrick for her."

Jarrett slung his own saddle onto the back of the California sorrel. "What's a Fitzpatrick?" he asked.

Driving a knee into the mare's side, Dev hauled on the latigo. "*The* Fitzpatrick. Her own true love."

"Huh?" Jarrett paused and stared at him.

"Her own true love," he repeated. "At least that's what she calls him. Her fiance, I reckon."

Jarrett whistled through his teeth. "You know, you got troubles. Old friend, if I was you I'd climb up on that pony and head west. I wouldn't stop but for water til I reached San Francisco."

"You don't know the half of it," Dev muttered to himself as he swung into the saddle.

Jarrett mounted and heeled the sorrel up beside him. "It's quite a town, San Francisco. Ever been there?"

"No."

"You don't know what living is til you've been to San Francisco. New Orleans ain't nothing compared to it. You ought to go sometime." He paused, then continued. "We could head out together."

When Dev didn't give him any reply, he added, "We could make a fair distance before nightfall."

"Likely." Dev caught up the lead rope on the buggy horse and gave it a tug as he touched heels to the mare's sides. "But I got unfinished business in Laramie."

X

The rain had finally stopped but high winds still whipped at the low-bellied clouds. And the town of Laramie seemed subdued by the damp weather. The walks weren't so crowded and the laughter wasn't so bright.

The two men came abreast of Bannerman's *Palace* and drew rein. Jarrett touched the brim of his hat. "I'll be leaving you here."

Dev nodded.

For a moment, Jarrett hesitated as if he were waiting for a reply of some kind. Then he nudged his horse toward the hitchrail. As he dropped rein over the rail, he gave Dev one last glance. Then he turned and pushed through the batwings.

When he was gone, Dev touched heels to

the mare's sides, moving her on toward the livery stable. She high-stepped through the mud and he had to pull at the lead rope to keep the buggy horse moving. As he rode through the open barn door, the swamper stepped out of an empty stall and looked him over narrowly. Eying the sorrel mare, he demanded, "Where's my buggy?"

"Busted up," Dev told him. "You can charge Hal Jarrett the price of it."

The old man worked his jaws and spat. Taking the lead rope from Dev's hand, he said skeptically, "Well, maybe Bannerman's good for it." He paused, squinting at Dev. "You're the buffalo skinner, ain't you?"

Dev nodded.

"There's a stranger in town lookin' for you. At least, he was asking your whereabouts."

"Who?"

"A stranger, damnit," he snapped. "Heavyset feller in a black fusty suit and a high collar to his shirt. Scruffy little beard. City feller, I'd say. Last I seen him, he was heading into Bannerman's place."

Who, Dev wondered. The description didn't fit anyone in particular. He nodded at the swamper as he turned his horse, and muttered, "Obliged."

"Don't thank me," the old man called

after him. "I wouldn't have told you except you brought back my horse."

Dev dismounted at the *Palace* and walked to the door. He shoved one batwing open and stood, looking around the room. The crowd was thinner than he'd seen it before but the smoke and noise were as intense as ever.

He spotted them — a heavyset fellow, obviously a city man, leaning on the bar and conversing with Dolph Bannerman. He wasn't sure how he knew — maybe he'd seen this one before or maybe it was just something about them that set them apart from ordinary people — but he recognized the man for what he was. A Pinkerton. He started to back out, then halted himself. Why run? The Pinks weren't after him. They were just tagging along, waiting for him to do something that would make it worthwhile to haul him back to a court of law in Illinois — like turning up with pocketfuls of that missing D.S. & F.M. money.

Was the Pink questioning Bannerman about a man named Devereaux, he wondered. Or just making casual talk in hope of picking up something worth his while? That was a favorite trick of theirs. And did Bannerman know the man was an agent?

Dev thought of the note of credit still

tucked in his pocket. A telegrapher's scrawl. Bannerman and Danforth had been partners for a long time. Could Bannerman have been the other man — the one on the Special before it derailed at Willis Siding? He pushed through the crowd toward them.

"Dev, I'm glad to see you," Bannerman called as he walked up. "This is Mister Vanarnam from New York. He's interested in buffalo hides and we've been talking a little business. It concerns you, or will if you're interested."

Dev nodded and the Pinkerton smiled sociably. "My pleasure, Mister . . . ?"

"Devereaux. Maybe you've heard the name before?"

The Pinkerton creased his face into a puzzled sort of frown. It looked almost convincing. He got back into his conversation with Bannerman as Dev called for a beer.

Picking up the mug, Dev glanced at the reflections in the bar mirror. Watching Bannerman's image, he rested his left hand on the bar and began to drum his fingers. It was a staccato, irregular tapping.

Bannerman turned to speak to the bartender and suddenly, in mid-word, he stopped. The eyes of his reflection met Dev's. They held for a moment and Dev could see the shock in them. Then he turned back to his conversation with Vanarnam. But there was no doubt that he'd read the message Dev had tapped out. And he'd been shaken by it.

Vanarnam's a Pinkerton. He knows about the wreck. That short message had held meaning for Bannerman. But what meaning? And which wreck would Bannerman think he'd meant, Dev wondered. Mike Conners, or the one at Willis Siding, or something else entirely?

He heard Bannerman's part of the conversation grow terse and after a moment break off altogether.

"Will you excuse me, Mister Vanarnam? I have something important to discuss with Devereaux."

The Pink nodded politely and Bannerman gestured for Dev to follow as he headed toward the stairs. Beer in hand, trying to look nonchalant, Dev trailed along. He could see the nervousness and concern in the set of Bannerman's shoulders and he knew that, for the moment at least, he had the advantage.

When Bannerman closed the office door behind them, he slipped the bolt. It snapped into place with a click that sounded uncommonly loud — and very final. Back to Dev, he walked to his place behind the big desk. When he turned there was an over-under sleeve gun in his hand. The muzzles made two very large black holes as he leveled it at Dev and asked, "Who are you?"

Half raising his hands, Dev fought the tension he felt. With a mock innocence, he answered, "Devereaux."

The corner of Bannerman's mouth twitched. Glancing at the Dragoon on Dev's thigh, he said, "Strip off that gun. Slow and easy with your left hand. And tell me what you are."

Dev dropped the gunbelt gently to the floor. The beer mug was still in his right hand and he sipped from it, trying to seem casual and unworried. Then he said, "Sometimes mule-skinner, sometimes hide-hunter."

"What is it you want with me?" Bannerman demanded. "What are you here for?"

"Don't you know?"

The slight nod of Bannerman's head suggested that he did know — or at least thought that he did. "The old man sent you, didn't he?"

Not Major Norstadt, Dev wondered. Did Bannerman know about his agreement with the major?

Bannerman looked pleased with himself,

139

as if in coming to some conclusion he'd gotten control over the situation. Almost smiling, he asked, "Did he send you to kill me, too?"

That didn't make sense, not if he meant the major. But who did he mean? Dev asked him, "What do you think?"

"I think he's a fool. I buried the last killer he sent in Julesburg. Doesn't he realize killing me won't get him anything? Those papers are in a safe place. If I died, Ruby'd still have them. And if anything happened to her, they'd fall into the hands of the law. I'm not going to kill you because I want you to take that message back to him. Tell him I've written out the whole story as sort of an insurance policy. If anything were to happen to me — to my wife — the whole story and the papers proving it would suddenly come to light. You understand?"

Dev looked at him blankly.

"Well, it doesn't matter whether or not *you* understand. You just take that message to him and *he'll* understand. He'd damned well better."

Dev nodded slowly, hoping he'd say something more. Something that might suggest who *he* was.

"That old fool," Bannerman muttered as if to himself, "letting the Pinks get this close. Doesn't he realize what would happen if they stumbled onto anything?"

"Maybe it wasn't *him* who sent the Pink," Dev said.

Bannerman looked puzzled. "But you said the Pink knew about the wreck at Willis Siding. . . . How else would he know . . . ?" He stopped short and gazed at Dev narrowly. "But you didn't say that, did you? You didn't say anything about Willis Siding . . . who are you, Devereaux?"

Dev started to frame an answer, but he was still talking, repeating the name to himself. And then he snapped, ". . . from Charlie Danforth! You're not from the old man. You're that damned telegrapher that Charlie . . ."

"Dolph!" someone shouted from the hallway.

Bannerman's head jerked toward the bolted door. And Dev flung the beer mug. He heard the gun go off as he threw himself down in front of the desk. He heard a fist hammering at the door. The voice was Hal Jarrett's, excited now, calling, "Dolph! What's the matter?"

Bannerman blinked. As he rubbed at his eyes, Dev lunged. His hands wrapped around Bannerman's wrist, wrenching at the little gun. He forced it back as the finger

141

on the trigger tightened and he heard the explosion, momentarily deafening, so close to his head. He eased his grip. The gun was empty now.

At the sound of the crash he wheeled. He saw the bolt half torn loose from the door frame and he saw the door shudder under another hard blow from Jarrett's boot. The bolt pulled futher out of the splintering wood.

Bannerman moved suddenly, grabbing for the Dragoon that lay on the floor. Lashing out, open-handed, Dev slammed the heel of his hand against the man's neck. As he crumpled forward, Dev grabbed for the gun-belt.

The door shuddered again and the bolt gave. As it was flung open, he saw Jarrett, his Colt in hand, and he spun, swinging the gunbelt with the heavy Dragoon in the holster. It slammed into Jarrett's chest, reeling him back into the hallway. The Colt bucked, plowing a slug into the ceiling, and Dev went in, under its muzzle.

His fists smashed into Jarrett's stomach and for an instant Jarrett's eyes met him. They seemed surprised — hurt — but as the fists struck, they went out of focus and Jarrett bent forward. Dev chopped at the back of his head and he sprawled face down.

142

Scooping up the gunbelt, Dev ran. As he hit the top of the stairway, he jerked to a stop. He'd heard two shots — from below.

He took a step down, listening to the hushed murmur of the people in the saloon, and bending, he looked out at them. They'd pressed back against the walls, making a clearing around the bar. There were two men in that clearing — Johnny Stark, standing gun in hand, and another lying on the floor, one outstretched hand still holding a revolver. The haze and smell of burnt gunpowder hung heavy over them.

Dev saw someone step from the crowd and reach down to turn over the body. The front of the butternut shirt had begun to stain red. The gaunt, gnarled old face was losing its color and the eyes that had been flat and secretive were completely blank. Jube Engels was dead.

Johnny Stark shook any loose bits of cap from his gun, holstered it, and turned back to his drink.

The piano player tapped a tentative note and then swung into a tune. Someone laughed. And the crowd broke.

Buckling the gunbelt around his waist, Dev continued down the stairs. He pushed hurriedly through the crowd and onto the street. He grabbed reins and swung up onto the calico mare, driving his heels into her sides. Bannerman would be on his trail. He was sure of that. He glanced back as he turned the corner. The mud sucked at the pony's hooves, then oozed back into each print, closing over it. She was leaving no sign. At least that much was in his favor.

She tried to turn off the street and he realized she wanted to head back into Bannerman's corral where she'd been fed and bedded before. He looked toward the corral, at the saddle horses there, picking out Jarrett's California sorrel, and thinking that having Bannerman after him would mean having Jarrett and Stark on his track as well. He touched rein to the mare's neck, heading her toward the corral. It would only take a minute, and it would slow them down a mite, he told himself.

At the gate, he jerked open the latch and then kneed the mare on in. With his rein ends, he gave the sorrel a slap on the rump that sent it skittering around the corral and out through the open gate. The other horses followed willingly.

There was one mount left. Bannerman's own horse stood tied inside the shed. He stepped down and edged into its stall. Jerking open the halter buckle, he waved his hands, sending the mount wheeling after the rest of the runaway horses. Then he started back for his mare. But a flick of motion caught his eye and he paused. Something had stirred under the crumpled wagon cover that was piled in a corner of the shed.

His hand moved to the butt of the Dragoon as he saw it move again. Drawing the gun, he reached out and jerked back the cloth.

She screamed.

It was a small, thin scream with almost no voice in it, but it scraped raw across his nerves. He grabbed her, his hand wrapping over her mouth, and hauled her to her feet.

She was like a wildcat struggling against him, her hands on his wrist, the nails digging into his flesh.

"Quiet," he said. "I won't hurt you!"

She stopped squirming and he eased his hand off her mouth. She tilted back her head, looking up at him. Her lupine-blue eyes were stark with fear, her face pale and tear-streaked. There was a large fresh bruise on her chin.

"Becky Engels," he said. She seemed to recognize him. As he let go, she threw herself down on the wagon cover. Pressing her face into her hands, she began to cry again.

He holstered the gun and dropped to one

knee. Gently, he put a hand on her shoulder. Her sobs were spasmodic and dry, as if she'd already cried out all her tears.

"Please — help me," she managed to say.

"How can I help?"

She turned quickly, looking at him. "Take me away!"

"Home?"

"No! Away — to New Orleans or San Francisco or Denver or anywhere *away* from here, away from him." She was gasping air into her lungs, but she wasn't crying anymore. "Please."

"You've got to go home now, Becky," he said softly. "Your family will need you now."

"No, no, no! They don't want me. They'll turn me out. When Paw finds out I've run away, he'll kill me."

When Paw finds out — then she didn't know her father was dead. That wasn't the reason she'd been huddled here crying. He told her, "Nobody's going to hurt you."

"*He* did. You see?" She put a hand to the bruise on her face.

"Your paw did that?"

She shook her head. "Johnny did it."

"Johnny?"

She nodded, pouting but yet looking almost proud, and said, "Johnny Stark."

"Why?"

"He's mine. I'm his woman. But then when I come here to him, he — he — please. . . ." She leaned her face against his shoulder, slipping an arm around his neck. "I ran away and come to him, but he hit me. I had to run away from him too."

"Come on," he said. He had to get her out of there before Stark showed up and found them both.

"You'll take me away? You'll take me to New Orleans?"

"I'll take you away from Stark."

She had both arms around his neck now. Pressing her face against his cheek, she said, "I like you."

He pulled free of her arms and helped her to her feet. Then he picked her up and set her on the calico pony, behind the cantle. As he settled into the saddle, she slipped her arms around his waist and leaned her head against his shoulder.

It had begun to rain again, and the mud was thick. The pony couldn't move fast through the streets, but once on the road, she found footing along the shoulder and he put her into a lope. She protested with a shaking of her head, but she stepped out, spattering mud over her belly and his legs with each stride. Even if she was half blind, he thought, she hadn't been such a bad bargain. She was a damned game mount. And bottom counted for a hell of a lot more than beauty.

He felt Becky's arm tighten around his waist and her hand against his ribs moved. She said, "You're strong, ain't you? Are you stronger than Johnny?"

He mumbled something unintelligible. How had she gotten mixed up with Stark, he wondered. Stark was Bannerman's man and Jube Engels hated Bannerman.

"Your shoulders are wider than his," her voice was softly dreamy. "Have you ever been to New Orleans?"

"No."

"Johnny promised he'd take me there. He promised me all kinds of things. He said I was pretty. Do you think I'm pretty?"

"Yes."

"Johnny said I was. He said I was as pretty as any of those fancy ladies, and he knows all about them."

"I'll bet he does."

"He ain't no ordinary old dirt-grubbing farmer like my folks," she went on. "He's real . . . real . . . he's from back East and his folks has got a big place with lots of horses and slaves and things. Least they did have up til the war. The Yankees burnt it all. That's how come him and Paw got on so good together. Paw says Johnny understands about how it is to have your home and crops burnt and to be run off your land."

There was no suggestion of sadness in her voice. She spoke in a slow, lazy way, as if she were half asleep or drifting in some waking dream. "But Johnny says he'll get back on top again. He's got it all planned out. He says he's gonna be the biggest man in Laramie someday. And then he's gonna go to New Orleans and be a big man there and make the name of Stark important like it was before the war. He promised to take me along so's I could be a fancy lady with pretty clothes and all."

Stark, Engels and Bannerman, Dev was thinking. And the railroad. He asked, "Your paw's friends with the Indians, ain't he?"

"Sure, there wasn't hardly nobody except Indians around here when we come out. But now there's that old railroad."

"Your paw's been helping the Indians make raids on the railroad, ain't he?"

"He hates the railroad," she said.

"Why?"

"It was a railroad took our land away, back in Illinois. Then railroad fellers come around and tried to buy it, only Paw said they was trying to steal it at that price and he run 'em off with his gun. Then they come back and burnt the house and everything and they told Paw they'd do worse if he didn't sign their old paper. So he done it and we got a big old wagon and come out here. It was nice here then. There wasn't no railroad for hundreds and hundreds of miles, Paw said."

"But now it's coming through here."

"It come after us like the Serpent in Eden." The way she said that, she was quoting her father. "It ruint everything. Paw stopped plowing and seeding, and all he does is ride with Lige and them Indians. And when he is home, he's mean and ugly and he hollers at me. Sometimes he hits me." She began to snuffle. "I hate him. I hate them all!"

He was mulling over the things she'd said, when suddenly she jabbed him in the ribs. Excitedly, she whispered, "There's somebody following us!"

XI

Dev glanced back over his shoulder. He saw nothing, but the girl whispered, "He's hid in the bushes. You reckon it's Paw?"

"No. You put your head down on my shoulder," he told her. "Pretend you're asleep. Don't let him know you've seen

150

him." He kept the horse moving at a steady pace. From the corner of his eye, he watched the brush. It seemed a long time before he caught a glimpse of motion, but once he'd spotted it, he was able to follow, approximating where the hidden rider would be.

Then he saw the man. Just for an instant, but it was time enough for him to identify the black Kossuth hat with the red-tipped feather in the band and to see that the man had a blanket wrapped around his shoulders. Laying rein along the mare's neck, he headed her off the wagon road, into the woods. There was a trail of sorts, leading in the direction of the Engels' place. And he had to get the girl home before trouble broke.

She straightened suddenly, demanding, "Where are you taking me?"

"Home."

"No!" She dug her nails into his ribs. "You're not taking me there. No you ain't!"

"I've got to get you to somewhere safe," he said.

She pounded a fist against his shoulder. "No, no, no!"

But he paid her no attention. He'd gotten the sudden feeling that the Breed was no longer behind them. He chanced glancing back, and then he was certain of it. Alert, he kept the pony moving, ignoring the girl's protests. What the hell had become of the Breed?

Something moved. He jerked his eyes toward the motion, stared at an outcropping of rocks ahead where the game trail turned downslope.

The Indian rose up before him. Evidently, he'd circled ahead when they turned onto the trail. He rose from the rocks, bareheaded with the blanket gone from his shoulders, and stood, naked to the waist. His wet black hair was plastered to his shoulders and the pale sundance scars glistened on his chest. The Spencer he held at his shoulder was pointed at Dev.

Grabbing at the girl, Dev dragged her down as he threw himself off the horse. He saw the rifle buck in the Breed's hands, heard the blast. And felt something hit him — hard.

He was on his knees in the mud, with the girl's arms tangled around his neck. He pushed her away as he cocked the Dragoon, aiming under the belly of the mare.

The horse had snorted, rearing at the gunshot and Dev's sudden jump. But in the instant he'd flung himself off her back, he'd given the reins a twist around his left wrist, Indian fashion, and the jerk of the bit had held her from bolting.

As he fired under her belly, she reared again, dragging at the reins. He felt the jerk at his wrist as a shock of pain and realized that he'd been hit. When he'd turned in the saddle, grabbing for the girl, the bullet aimed for his chest had struck his arm. Digging his teeth into his lip, he tried to get his fingers around the reins, to pull back the mare's head and ease the jerking. But the hand wouldn't work, the fingers wouldn't move.

The pony went higher, pawing at the sky and he dug his teeth deeper into his lip, fighting the pain. It washed over him, almost drowning his awareness of the Breed. He fought it. Steadying the heavy Colt in his good hand, he sighted on the Indian's bare chest.

The Breed was levering another cartridge into the Spencer's chamber. Or was he? Dev saw his hand jerk at the lever and jerk again. It was an angry, nervous motion, and Dev realized the rifle had jammed.

Bracing his elbow against his knee, he took aim and squeezed the trigger of the Colt. The instant between the pull and the explosion of the cap seemed interminably long, his hand impossibly unsteady. Finally the six-gun bucked.

He saw the Breed jerk, dropping back behind the rocks. Had he scored? He couldn't be sure. The mare was struggling against the bit again, dragging at his arm and pulling his mind away from the Breed. He had to get himself free of the horse. With his right hand, he grabbed at the reins, close to the bit. Swinging his weight against it, he managed to haul her head down. The pain eased.

Something was moving in the rocks. He saw the Breed glance out. But he didn't see the muzzle of the Spencer. Clinging to the reins, he shouted, "Your medicine's no good. Your gun's busted. Your woman will be cutting her hair for you tonight."

The Breed jerked his head down. But Dev's shout had startled the frightened horse, too, and she tried to rear again. Clutching the reins close to the bit, he turned his attention to calming her. A sound from the rocks pulled his gaze back, but he saw nothing of the Breed. And then he heard hooves — a horse was being ridden away fast. The Breed was superstitious.

Slowly, the mare steadied. As he spoke to her, she turned her head and studied him, her one good eye rolling, showing the white. She flared her nostrils and snorted, but finally she stood steady.

He bit at the reins wrapped around his wrist, jerked them loose with his teeth. His hand, his whole arm, throbbed. For a long moment, he leaned against the horse, drawing deep breaths. Then he straightened and looked at his coat sleeve. There was a small hole in the wet canvas between the elbow and the shoulder. He couldn't see any blood. When he tried to turn his arm, to look closer, it wouldn't move.

"Devereaux!" The girl's voice was high and thin. She sat in the mud, holding the gun he'd dropped in his fight with the horse.

She had to use both hands to raise it up, and the muzzle quavered as she leveled it at him. Fiercely she said, "If you try to take me back home, I'll kill you."

He might have cursed at her. But he felt too damned tired to be bothered. He said, "It don't shoot if it ain't cocked."

She put her thumb to the hammer and tried to haul it back. The gun was far too big for her hand. She could barely span the hammer and could get no leverage against it. She tried with both thumbs and almost dropped it.

He watched with the patience of exhaustion as she struggled with the heavy Dragoon. She'd begun to cry again, angry frustrated sobs that shook her whole body.

Suddenly she threw the gun down and bowed her head.

Dev bent and picked up the gun. It was sopping with mud. He wiped it across his thigh, then dropped it back into the holster. "Becky," he said, but she didn't look toward him. "Becky, get up."

"No," she mumbled. "You can't take me home. I won't go. Paw'll kill me."

He thought of telling her then that her father was dead. But it was too hard a thing. He couldn't just speak it out. He said, "Then I'll take you somewheres else. Just get up and give me a hand."

She raised her face, her eyes widening hopefully, and she smiled. "New Orleans?"

He felt a sudden flush of disgusted anger. Whatever troubles she had, they'd be of her own making. If she'd stayed away from Johnny Stark, stayed home where she'd belonged . . . but what the hell good are "ifs"? Bracing himself against the horse, he fingered at the buttons of the surcoat. "Becky, give me a hand," he repeated.

Her eyes were on him, but she did not move.

He got the buttons open and manged to shrug his right arm out of the coat. Carefully, he worked the sleeve down over his injured arm. He flung the coat over the saddle and clung to the pommel for a moment, steadying himself. Then he looked at the arm. The drizzle washed at the stain that was smearing over his shirtsleeve and the blood that trickled down his limp hand.

The hole seemed small for the amount of blood that was coming out of it. He had to get the bleeding stopped. Funny how a man's life could run out through a little hole like that. Again, he asked the girl for help.

She was sniffling. For a moment her eyes held on his. They were red-rimmed and vacant, and he knew she wouldn't move. One-handed, he worked loose his neckerchief and somehow he got it wrapped tight around the arm. Somehow, using his good hand and his teeth, he got it knotted.

It felt as if the bone were broken, and the arm sure needed support of some kind. He used his belt for a sling and once he got his hand through it, the pain eased off a bit. He needed help getting the coat over his shoulders but he had none. It was useless to even ask the girl. Once he'd fumbled the top button closed at his throat, he had to lean against the horse again, to keep on his feet. He felt exhausted, ready to lie down and let life seep away. He shook his head, trying to clear his thoughts. He had to get onto that horse and keep going. He focused his attention on that thought. Studying the girl huddled at his feet, he said, "Get up and get on this horse."

She pressed her face deep into her hands. "I can't!"

"Then stay here," he muttered. Grabbing the saddlehorn, he hauled himself up onto the mare.

"No!" Becky shouted as she scrambled to her feet. "Don't leave me!"

"Then get on."

"Help me," she snuffled.

Wearily, he held out his good hand to her. She took hold and struggled up behind him. It seemed to take her a damned long time.

As he touched heels to the pony's sides, she begged, "Please don't take me back home. Take me anywhere else, but not back there."

She was like a child, he thought. A frightened, self-centered, half-witted child. Where could he take her? Where could he take himself? He knew he'd lost a lot of blood and was losing more. He had to have help. A doctor, maybe. Where could he go? He remembered the big, bony-faced doctor. Of course, he could go back to Sullivan's.

As he turned the horse, he mumbled, "All right, I won't take you back home."

She slipped her arm around his waist

again. Her hand moved over his ribs caressingly. Her voice soft and dreamy, she asked once more, "Will you take me to New Orleans?"

The sky had darkened from gray to black and the wind kept whipping at the thin drizzle as they rode. The mare was plodding now, throwing its hooves, struggling through the mud in the road.

Sullivan's couldn't be much further, Dev thought. It seemed like he'd been riding forever. He wondered if he could have missed the turn-off in the dark and gone too far up the wagon trail. He thought he remembered making the turn-off. But it was so damned dark. And the girl, sleeping with her head on his shoulder, was a dead weight.

He frowned, listening. Had he heard a dog, or dreamed it? Yes, he heard it again. With a sigh, he urged the pony on. And suddenly a light appeared, filling a window with its warm, yellow glow. It was close. Closer than he'd judged from the sound of the dog. The door opened and Sullivan was silhouetted in it. His face took form as he raised a lantern. "Who is it?" he called. "Devereaux?"

It struck Dev funny — Sullivan standing there in his nightshirt calling his name into

159

the darkness. Had the man come to expect his sudden arrivals in the middle of the night?

"Yeah, it's me," he called back as he reined the pony into the circle of lantern light.

Sullivan squinted at him. "What's happened now? Who's that with you?"

Before Dev could answer, the girl slid down and was running toward Sullivan. She threw herself against him, wrapping her arms around his neck and whimpering, "Please, please help me!"

He pried her loose and asked gently, "What's the matter?"

"She's run off from home and she's looking for somebody to take her to New Orleans," Dev said. As he eased himself down off the horse, Mrs. Sullivan's face appeared in the doorway.

"What's the matter? Oh, Mister Devereaux . . ." She saw Becky and asked, "Who's this?"

"A stray. She's — she's —" The dizziness swelled over him. He had to grab at the saddle to support himself.

"You're hurt!" he heard Mrs. Sullivan say. She was hurrying toward him.

"Caught a ball in my arm," he muttered. "Reckon I lost some blood."

Sullivan handed the lantern to his wife and got Dev's good arm over his shoulder. With the man's help, he got to the kitchen and once he was sitting down, he felt better. But the whiskey Sullivan gave him just set his head to spinning again.

He lost track of what was going on around him. He was aware of Mrs. Sullivan taking Becky Engels into another room, and of the Sullivan boy being sent to fetch the doctor. He knew that Sullivan asked him what had happened and that his answer was incoherent, but it didn't seem to matter. The only thing that mattered, the only thing he wanted in the world, was to put his head down, close his eyes and sleep. But he had a notion he couldn't let himself do that.

"Here now," he heard Mrs. Sullivan saying, her voice like something in a dream. He felt her hand on his face. She was trying to give him something to drink. He sipped at it and the scalding heat of the bitter, black coffee cut through the haze in his mind.

He saw her broad face in front of him and she was smiling, but there was a deep furrow of concern between her brows. "Here now," she repeated, "drink this and you'll feel better."

He drank more of the coffee and then she

dabbed at his face with a cold damp cloth while Sullivan cut the shirtsleeve away from his wounded arm. She was right. The coffee did make him feel better. He drank more of it. And over the rim of the cup, his eyes focused on Maury O'Neil.

She stood framed in a doorway, with a bright blue robe clutched around her shoulders and the coppery hair tumbling loose around her face. "You're hurt," she said.

Mrs. Sullivan turned at the sound of her voice. "Maury, you shouldn't be up on your feet."

As if she hadn't heard, the girl kept looking at Dev.

"Is it bad?" she asked.

"No," he answered.

"If you insist . . ." Mrs. Sullivan was muttering as she helped Maury to a chair. When the girl asked her for a cup of coffee, she protested. "It'll keep you awake."

"How can a body sleep with *him* gallivanting around making a racket to raise the Dear?" Maury said, with a nod toward Dev. She accepted the cup Mrs. Sullivan held out to her and sipped from it. Looking down into the cup, she added, "He comes and he goes and he comes back, one time with a new shirt and then again with a bullet in him. And who's to know if he'll come back again."

She sounded angry. He mumbled, "I don't intend to get myself killed, if that's what you mean."

"And was it your intention to get yourself shot at all?"

"No." It seemed damned unfair of her to be angry and argue now when he couldn't think straight enough to answer for himself.

"If you'd the sense of a suckling pig, you'd give up whatever wild goose it is you're chasing," she said. "You'd settle down to something like honest work — with a railroad."

"I did work for a railroad once."

"And you gave it up?" She made it sound like something no sane man could do.

He asked himself why he'd told her that. And he decided to go and tell her the rest of it — get it over with. "I was blacklisted," he said.

Frowning, she shaped the word with her lips.

He nodded. And then he told her. He knew he was doing a bad job of explaining it. His thoughts were muddled and he kept feeling like he'd left out things, or repeated himself. But he got it all spread out in words for her. He finished off by explaining his suspicions of Bannerman.

"That's the wild goose I'm chasing," he said.

She was thoughtfully silent for a long moment. Then she asked, "When you've caught it, will you come back to the railroad?"

She'd accepted the story, he thought with a giddy elation. She did believe it. He caught rein on himself — there was still the Fitzpatrick, her own true love. She had her plans and she was happy with them. Did he have any right . . . ? He told himself he damned well did have the right at least to tell her how he felt about her. The decision was hers to make. But he had the right to tell her — she had the right to know.

He met her eyes and said it. "I'm in love with you."

She jerked her head, looking away from him, and her face reddened. "Mister Devereaux!" She sounded properly indignant. And then she smiled, looking at him from under her lashes, and said softly, "Well, you've taken your own time getting to saying it, haven't you?"

"You knew . . . ?"

"Why shouldn't I? Since I've the same feeling. . . ."

Mrs. Sullivan made a point of clearing her throat. As he glanced toward her, Dev asked, "The Fitzpatrick?"

"He'll be agreeable," Maury said. "And if he's not, he'll have no say in the matter."

"But I thought you — he —" He stumbled over the words, but she understood.

Tactfully, she told him, "It may be true that Fitzpatrick's my Uncle and my Guardian, but my life is my own, and there are things I'll decide for myself."

He laughed. He couldn't help it. How could he have been such a damn fool as to worry himself, to think of riding out without ever speaking his mind . . . ?

"Horse coming," Sullivan said suddenly. He leaned his head out the door. "The doctor."

XII

He was strangling. Coughing, Dev forced his eyes open. He found he was gagging on the whiskey the doctor was trickling into his mouth. As he focused on the man's bony, weathered face, it spread into a grin.

"That's better," the doctor said.

"What is?" Dev managed to say. The effort set him to coughing again.

"You," Bloch answered. He held up a lump of lead between his thumb and forefinger. "Want this as a souvenir? Or do you already have a collection of them?"

"No, thanks. I'd rather just forget it," Dev answered. He'd finally caught his breath. Glancing around, he decided this was the boy's room the Sullivans' had bedded him down in. He moved his good arm, trying to prop himself on it and sit up.

The doctor pressed a heavy hand on his chest, forcing him down. "Hold still. You want to ruin my handiwork?"

Tucking his chin, Dev tried to look at the bandage wrapped around his upper arm and his chest. The arm was strapped tight against his side.

Following his gaze, the doctor explained, "That's to keep you from moving it. Got to keep the bone in place while it knits. I did a damned good job there. Treat it right and it'll heal clean. Be as good as ever."

Looking at Bloch's hand on his chest, Dev asked, "How long you plan on holding me down?"

The doctor shrugged. "Well, the knitting should be firm in about four to six weeks. Depends on how fast your body heals. Of course you won't be confined to bed the whole time. Maybe only a week or so."

"Like hell," Dev grunted.

Bloch nodded sadly. "I've had patients like you before. Damned waste of time trying to do a decent job. Why can't at least one of you show a little sense and lie still. You should at least get a good night's sleep before you go disobeying my orders." He lifted the hand tentatively a little above Dev's chest. With grinning sarcasm, he added, "You see, you can lie still if you've a mind to."

"Not for any four to six weeks I can't."

"Who's after you?"

"Dolph Bannerman and his friends."

Bloch whistled softly between his teeth. "Well, that's nice. When you pick your enemies you go first class, don't you? This his?" He tossed the bullet in the palm of his hand.

"That half-breed that works for him," Dev said.

"Well, I can see where I won't be able to keep you down long," Bloch said with a sigh. "But you've lost a lot of blood. You're weak. If you try to haul out of here tonight, you'll probably be killing yourself, you know."

"I know."

The doctor sighed again. "Sit up," he said, offering Dev a hand. "I'll put a little more plaster on that arm. Bind it so you can ride without busting it apart again. Then I'll give you something to help you sleep. You eat regularly and rest as much as you can and

167

don't lose any more blood, maybe you'll survive."

The doctor's hands were big and thick-knuckled, but they worked with a quick confidence and his touch was light. When he'd finished, he grunted, "That ought to hold up for you to ride. Hell, it'll hold up if you fall off."

"I ain't planning to fall off, thanks."

"Mind you don't. And no thanks necessary. Just keep bringing me your business. With a practice consisting of you and your friends, I'll retire in luxury in a few years." As he spoke, Bloch mixed something in a glass. He held it out and said, "Drink it all."

Dev swallowed the stuff. It was sharply bitter. As he handed back the empty glass, he asked, "What'll that do?"

"Keep you quiet a while so nature can work on that arm." Bloch turned toward Sullivan. "Keep him down as long as you can. Now, I think I'd better take a look at that girl he brought in."

"That you'd better," Mrs. Sullivan agreed. "The poor girl was tuckered out and soaked to the skin. Come on, I'll show you. . . ."

"Mrs. Sullivan," Dev said as she reached for the lamp. "That girl, Becky Engels. Somebody's got to tell her. I couldn't, not the way things were. Maybe you can, being

168

you're a woman. . . ."

"Tell her what?"

"Her father's dead. Johnny Stark shot him down in the *Palace* this afternoon."

"Oh, my dear!" Her eyes widened. She picked up the lamp and followed her husband and the doctor out of the room, shaking her head slowly and mumbling, "The poor child. . . ."

Dev remembered the way he'd seen the girl back at her house, standing there on the porch, looking down at her own brother's dead body with an excited but impersonal curiosity. He wondered if she'd cry for her father.

It was the barking of the dog that woke him. He lay gazing at the rafters, feeling as if he were still adrift in a dream. He could hear the hoofbeats of an approaching horse and he wondered idly if it was the doctor coming back, in the saddle this time. There was no creak of a buggy. And then he heard the rider hallo the house. The voice was Hal Jarrett's.

The sense of dreaming broke. Starkly awake, he grabbed at the bedstead with his good hand and sat up. As he swung his legs over the edge of the mattress, his head spun. He closed his eyes against the dizziness, then opened them and tried to focus. The indigo denim of his pantslegs was just a blue blur.

Slowly his sight sharpened. He glanced around, looking for the rest of his clothes. The surcoat was hanging over the back of a chair and his boots were nearby. Holding onto the bedpost, he got to his feet and headed unsteadily toward the chair. Why so damned weak? he wondered. Was it that draught the doctor had given him? Would it wear off? How soon?

He picked up the coat and found his gunbelt underneath it, looped over the chairback. The big Dragoon was in the holster, just as he'd left it — caked with mud. Until it had been cleaned and reloaded it was useless. And even if he'd had the time, he couldn't clean and load a gun with one hand. But there wasn't any time. Through the closed door, he could hear the murmur of voices, and he knew Jarret was in the kitchen.

He got the boots on and the coat draped over his shoulders. Wearily, he rubbed a hand across his face. Then he stepped to the door and edged it open.

Jarrett was standing near the table, grinning as he talked with Mrs. Sullivan. He had his hat in one hand and a thin bunch of flowers in the other. They were half-open Columbine buds, bright blue and fresh-picked. He gestured with them as he talked.

"Morning, Hal," Dev said.

Surprise flashed across Jarrett's face. Then he nodded, glancing at the bandages, and said, "You shoulda gone to San Francisco. What happened?"

"The Breed followed me out of Laramie but his rifle jammed." Dev's voice was level but edged with tension. "Did Bannerman send you here to finish the job?"

"I don't reckon Dolph knows you're here. I sure didn't."

"Has he told you he wants me dead?"

Jarrett nodded.

"Now?"

"Why? You in some kind of a hurry?" Keeping his eyes on Dev, he set his hat down on the table, then put the bouquet gently beside it. Cocking his head slightly, he said, "You ain't wearing a gun?"

"No."

"Seems like you never got one when you need it," he mumbled. Without moving his eyes away from Dev he reached for the tie-down that held his holster. He jerked it loose, then unbuckled the gunbelt and laid it on the table next to the flowers. "Hell, I got my pride. I got me a reputation to uphold." He sounded almost apologetic.

Mrs. Sullivan glanced anxiously from one to the other. "You! Both of you, you're acting like — like a couple of bull calves just budding horns. Now, you'll sit down to that table and have a bite of breakfast, the both of you, and behave like gentlemen or I'll take the bald-headed end of the broom to the pair of you!"

They looked at her and then at each other. Suddenly Jarrett's face spread into a wide grin. "Yes'm," he said docilely as he pulled out a chair and settled into it.

Dev felt the tension ease out of his shoulders. He grinned back at Jarrett and then began to laugh. Jarrett laughed too. And at that, so did Mrs. Sullivan.

But it wasn't funny — not at all. When he caught his breath, he looked at Jarrett and said soberly, "Hal, it was the Breed that shot Maury O'Neil."

Hal stopped laughing. "I figured that out."

"Why'd he do it? What reason could he have had for going after her?"

He eyed Dev curiously. "You."

"Me?"

"Ruby seen you out her window when you came back into town with her from Nash's. She ain't been able to figure out why you act the way you do with her and she reckoned it must've been on account of that redheaded girl," he said. "So she sent the Breed after her, to get her out of the way. Breed followed me and her, and took his chance when he got it. He wasn't after no horse nor scalp neither. Just her."

Dev ran a hand across his face. "How the hell could Ruby . . . ?"

"Ruby's real used to getting whatever she wants."

"Well, I reckon Bannerman's changed his mind about getting her me," Dev mumbled. "Way he sent the Breed after me yesterday. . . ."

"Wasn't Dolph who sent him. He's Ruby's hand," Hal told him. "Was her wanted you shot. You got her upset something awful."

"Huh?"

"Never was anything she wanted that she couldn't get until you come along. First she thought it was on account of that redheaded girl. Then yesterday, she got a look at you riding out of town with some other girl up behind of your saddle. I reckon that was too much for her — seemed to her like you'd take up with anything in skirts except her. Lordy, I never seen her so mad."

"Did she see who the girl was?" Dev asked.

"I don't know. She just told the Breed to

take out after you and kill you both. Then she run off crying and locked herself in her room. She wouldn't even let Dolph in. I never seen her that way before." He picked up his cup and gulped at the coffee. As he put it down again he mumbled, "She never carried on none like that for me."

Mrs. Sullivan had kept to her stove, with her back to them. If she'd listened to what was said, she didn't comment as she set plates of food in front of them. Then she turned back, to busy herself at the stove again.

Jarrett stared at the plate of eggs and prodded them with his fork. He didn't seem very interested in them. Suddenly he looked up, his dark eyes serious. "Damnit, Dev! Life around here was all plain and simple and easy till you came along. Now it's all a mess from one end to the other. Why the hell don't you light a shuck for California or somewhere? Get out of Laramie and leave us all alone?" He reached for a pocket. "If you need money, I got a fair piece I . . ."

"I've still got business in Laramie," Dev said, "with Dolph Bannerman."

"Why? What did Dolph ever do to you?"

"Name of Willis Siding mean anything to you?"

Frowning, Jarrett shook his head. "Not as

174

I recall. Where is it?"

"Illinois."

"You knew Dolph when he was in Illinois?"

"No," Dev told him, "but I knew Charlie Danforth there."

"Charlie's dead. Stark killed him. And he'll kill you, too. If it ain't Johnny who does it, it'll be the Breed or Dolph himself or maybe me. You ain't got a chance with odds like that. Get smart and haul your tail out'n this part of the country before Dolph finds out where you're holed up." He tugged one of the flowers out of the bouquet and rolled the stem between his fingers. With a sharp thrust of his thumbnail, he snapped off the blossom.

Dev looked at it, lying next to the holstered Colt. Then he looked at Jarrett. "If Bannerman didn't know I was here, what'd you come here for?"

Grinning sheepishly, he answered, "I kinda come calling on that redheaded girl. Hell, you don't think I'd bring posies if I come calling on you, do you?"

"You stay the hell away from Maury O'Neil!"

He looked surprised, a little hurt. "I gotta apologize to her or something," he mumbled. "I'm mixed up in all this, seeing

175

it was on account of me she was out there alone. But it was Ruby who sent the Breed and I couldn't raise a hand against Ruby. Not no how."

"You stay away from Maury O'Neil," Dev repeated, his voice hard.

"That ain't your right to say." Hal turned to Mrs. Sullivan. "It's the girl's right to say, ain't it, Ma'm? She's the one to say whether she'll see me or not, ain't she?"

The woman nodded slowly. "It's her right to say," she echoed. Then she smiled. "It's high time she was awake. Maybe she'll be seeing you both." She hurried through the bedroom door.

After a moment, she returned, her face creased in puzzlement. "Mister Devereaux, that little girl you brought in last night — she's gone."

"What!"

"She slipped out while Maury was asleep."

Dev shoved open the kitchen door and looked out. The sun was well up and bright. Under it, the still damp earth held sharp clear prints of small feet heading for the barn and of a horse leaving it.

"She's took my pony," he muttered as he turned back. "Mrs. Sullivan, you got a horse I could take the loan of?"

"Why the Mister and the boy have both

176

rode out to tend our stock. I reckon they've got both horses. 'Sides, you're not strong enough to go riding after anybody."

"I've got to fetch her back." Dev looked toward Jarrett.

"Oh no! Not my horse. . . ."

Dev's right hand shot out, his fingers wrapping around the butt of his Colt on the table. He jerked it out of the holster and leveled it as he thumbed back the hammer.

Jarrett raised his hands automatically. His black brows met as he frowned in surprise. "Don't be a damn fool, Dev."

"I need her back," Dev said, backing toward the door.

"Not with my own gun . . ." he heard Jarrett mutter, as he wheeled, slamming the door behind him.

He shoved the Colt into his waistband and grabbed at the California sorrel's reins. As he swung into the saddle, his head spun again. But in a moment the dizziness had passed and he realized with relief that his strength was coming back. He kicked his heels into the horse's sides and turned from the house at a gallop.

In the drying mud the sign was easy to follow. The girl had walked the pony away from Sullivan's, and once she was out of earshot, she'd put it into a gallop, heading straight back toward her home.

He thought about the stubborn way she'd resisted being taken back there the night before. Now she was headed that way. Then he remembered asking Mrs. Sullivan to tell her that Jube Engel was dead. He had a strong notion she hadn't cried for her father.

The sorrel was a damn fine horse. From the look of the tracks he was gaining on the girl. Maybe he'd be able to catch up. He had to get her back and take her to Major Nordstadt. The major had questions that Becky Engels could answer.

He'd almost reached the rim of Engels' valley when he finally caught sight of her. For an instant he glimpsed her on the crest of the rise. And then she was gone, down into the valley.

He followed, halting the sorrel on the ridge. He could see her below, dropping off the pony and running up onto the porch. He was too late.

He sat there, looking at the house, wondering what to do now. And suddenly he heard a sound behind him. It was the cracking of a branch, followed close by the cocking of a gunhammer.

As his shoulders stiffened, he heard the voice. "All right, Wrecker. Raise up them hands where I can see 'em or give me a good excuse to put a ball through your gizzard."

He looked at the house a moment longer, then wearily gave the reins a twist around the saddlehorn and raised his good hand.

Brush crackled and a man appeared to his right. Then another came up on his left. Bewildered, he glanced from one to the other. They were soldiers.

"He's the one, ain't he, Corporal Stiles?" the voice behind him asked.

The corporal nodded. "No doubt. He fits the description."

"Except for the arm," his companion said. "General Jack didn't say anything about his arm."

"Maybe we winged him yesterday," Stiles suggested.

"Maybe you've got the wrong man," Dev said hopefully.

Stiles looked at him, eyes narrowed. "You're Devereaux, aren't you? The *buffalo skinner?*" He put a strange, sarcastic emphasis on his words.

Dev nodded.

"Take his gun, McInerney," the corporal told his companion.

The soldier sidled his horse up beside the pony and jerked the Colt from Dev's waistband. He handed it to Stiles.

The corporal nodded, then called out to the man behind Dev: "Brown, you ride behind and keep him covered. If he makes a move, kill him."

"What's this all about?" Dev asked.

Stiles seemed smugly pleased as he replied, "General Casement wants to have a talk with you."

XIII

General Jack Casement was seated at his desk in the field office tent. He leaned back in his chair, watching as Corporal Stiles brought his party to a halt and ordered Dev to dismount. Executing a brisk salute, the corporal said, "We caught him at the Engels place, General."

Casement got to his feet. "Somebody fetch Major Nordstadt over to my waycar. You come along with me, Devereaux. I want to talk to you."

As they walked through the camp, Dev saw workers stop and gaze at him sullenly. Judging from the hostility they showed, the whole camp had him labeled now as a wrecker. What had happened, he wondered. How had they found out?

The general's waycar, like Major Nordstadt's, was a converted caboose. But it was bigger, more modern and more cluttered. Casement picked up a map off a chair, thrust it into an already-tottering pile of papers, and seated himself behind the desk. He steepled his fingers and gazed over them at Dev.

Leaning against the closed door, Dev looked back at him and asked, "General, just what am I accused of?"

Casement raised his brows questioningly. The furrow between them deepened. Wordlessly, he dug into a desk drawer and brought out a folded paper. He spread it on the desk and shoved it toward Dev. It was an old newspaper clipping — an account of the investigation into the wreck at Willis Siding.

Dev looked at his own name in the crowded columns of thick black type. "Where did this come from?"

"We had company here in camp last night," Casement told him. "Some teamster from Laramie happened by. He also *happened* to have this with him. He left it with one of our men."

"A Bannerman driver?"

The general nodded.

"So Bannerman's decided to have your track layers lynch me."

"Why would he want that?" Casement

181

asked. The question was a probe.

"The major's told you, hasn't he?" Dev said. When the general nodded, he asked, "Do you believe any of it?"

"I'll listen to you."

Dev started at the sound of footsteps outside the car. He stepped away from the door as someone knocked, and Casement called, "Come in."

It was Major Nordstadt. He looked at Dev and at the bandages. "What happened to you?"

"I got myself shot. Major, this Board of Directors' meeting that J. B. Hendon was on his way to when he was wrecked at Willis Siding" — Dev picked up the clipping and held it out — "have you got any idea what it was about?"

"A very confidential matter. Why?"

"Was it an investigation? Into something funny going on within the corporation or something like that?"

"Why?" the major repeated.

"Because Dolph Bannerman was Danforth's partner in that wreck. And there was a third man involved. Hendon lost a lot of his books and records in that fire, didn't he?"

"What the hell are you getting at, Dever-

182

eaux?" Casement demanded, rising to his feet.

"If Hendon was taking records of some kind to Chicago, to that board meeting for an investigation, then I think I know what happened," Dev told him. "The way I piece it together, Bannerman has those records, or at least the most important ones. Instead of burning all the papers, the way he was supposed to, he stole them along with the money. Since then he's been blackmailing Hendon with them. If I can get my hands on them, they'll hang Hendon. And clear me."

Shaking his head incredulously, Casement sat down again.

Major Nordstadt was frowning. "You're sure of this, Dev? It's a strong accusation."

"I'm damned sure. And I figure to get hold of proof to back up the accusation."

"What about this business yesterday?" Casement said.

Dev asked, "What happened yesterday?"

"Somebody tried to fire the trestle at Grennell Creek," the major told him. "Our boys spotted them, though, before they could do any damage."

"Not the Lakota?"

"No, white men. Two of them."

"You figured I was one?"

"A lot of the men who saw this clipping did," Casement answered. "We found one of the two in the woods near the trestle, but the other got away."

"The one we found was dead," Major Nordstadt added. "There was a ball in his back. But it wasn't us who got him. We found powder marks on his coat around the bullethole. And this was on the ground not far away." He picked up a six-gun from among the papers on the desk and handed it to Dev. It was a Remington Navy Model.

He turned it in his hands, studying it. The butt plates were carved bone, the cylinder and frame were covered with fine engraving. Entwined in the decoration along the top strap was a name — A. Bannerman.

"Who was the dead man?" he asked as he handed the gun back.

"Elijah Engels. Our men figured . . ."

"General," Dev interrupted. "You'd better get those bluecoats up to the Engels' place and look after the womenfolk. If it isn't too late already. He'll for sure plan to kill them too."

Responding to the urgency in Dev's voice, Major Nordstadt leaned out the door, calling to someone outside. He gave hurried orders and then turned back to Dev. "Who'll kill them?"

"Johnny Stark."

Running a thumb over the top strap of the Remington, the general said, "Well, we figured it would be either Bannerman himself or some one of his hired killers."

Dev asked, "You thought it was me on account of that clipping and on account of I had hired on with Bannerman?"

"I will admit the thought crossed my mind."

"Why would Stark murder Lige Engels and then kill the women?" Major Nordstadt asked.

"He killed Jube last night. That wasn't anything he planned, though," Dev said. "Engels' daughter ran away after him and I suppose the old man must have trailed her to the *Palace*. From what I saw Jube braced Stark. I talked to the girl and she pretty much admitted her father was the white man who's been encouraging the Indian raids, but I think Stark was in on that too."

"Stark killed Lige because of the girl?" Nordstadt asked skeptically.

"I think he killed Lige because he was afraid when Lige heard about his father's death, he'd turn on Stark and expose the whole thing. Now he'll be out to kill the women for the same reason."

"I don't understand," Casement said.

185

"What about Bannerman? He's the one who's been engineering these raids, isn't he?"

"Not the way I see it," Dev answered. "I think Stark was using Engels and his hatred for the railroad against Bannerman. He's got a notion he can take over Bannerman's property and his wife, if he can get Dolph out of the way. He can't kill the man outright, so he figured on making it look like Bannerman was responsible for the raids. Likely, he got hold of that gun you've got there and used it to kill Lige with the intention that you blame Bannerman for the raid and the murder."

Shaking his head, Casement leaned down and pulled a brandy flask out of the bottom desk drawer. He uncorked it and took a drink. Then he shoved it toward Dev. "Maybe you'd better sit down and tell me this whole thing from the beginning."

There was a hand on his shoulder and a voice calling, "Devereaux, wake up."

Dev opened his eyes and looked at Major Nordstadt. The lamp was turned low and the interior of the major's car was twilight-dark. Shadows from the lamp deepened the creases of the major's frown.

"What's the matter?" Dev asked.

"I'm sending you back to Sullivan's. Noah's gone for the horses. He'll ride with you. I've told him everything." The major was holding a gun. It was Jarrett's Navy Colt. He handed it to Dev.

As he took it, Dev asked again, "What's the matter?"

"Somebody's been circulating whiskey around the camp," the major explained. "And gossip too. The hands are getting in an ugly mood. I don't like the way they're talking. I want to get you out of the camp."

"Bannerman's whiskey?"

"How the hell should I know? I suppose so. You can hole up at Sullivan's. I'll drive up in the morning and we can decide what to do next. I may have to send you out on the next train back to Omaha."

"I'm not running, Major," Dev said as he tucked the gun into his waistband. "I'm too close to quit now. I've told you what's happened. I know that Bannerman is the one I'm after. All I need is proof — something here in my hand that I can show."

"I've got connections and influence. I can use them to get a real investigation started. The important thing right now is to get you out of here."

"There's already been an investigation," he answered the major. "Besides, that's only part of it now. There's Maury O'Neil, too. She and I — well — it was kinda my fault she got shot and I mean to kill the man who did it."

"Do you know who it was?"

He nodded.

The major looked thoughtfully at him. "Well, you're of age. The decision is yours to make."

"I intend . . ." Dev cut himself short as the waycar door opened. It took a moment for him to recognize the shabbily-dressed old man who stood there, hat in hand, as Noah Freedman.

"I brought the horses," Noah said. "We'd better get going."

Cocking his head, Dev gestured at Noah's coat and the limp wool hat. "Why?" he asked.

"We're going through the camp guards as quietly as we can," Noah answered. "I'd rather they don't notice us. And there's no telling who we might run into on the road. We could run into trouble. . . ."

"Besides, it's been a long time since Noah ran contrabands through the lines," the major added with a grin. "He was just aching to try his hand at a little subterfuge again."

Noah grinned himself and nodded. "Come

on, I've got the horses right outside."

"Take care of yourself," the major called as Dev followed the old man out the door.

They walked, leading the horses, until they were past the lines of the railroad's night guards. Then they mounted up and set the horses into a ground-covering lope. The moon gave good light to the wagon road, and it was easy traveling.

When they halted to let the mounts catch breath, Dev said, "Noah, you're good. Hell, if I was out to steal a few ponies, I couldn't ask for a better man to go with me. You came through that line as quiet as any Skisika."

"It's a skill I learned on the underground railway," Noah told him. "A man has to be able to move silently in work like that. I'll tell you an interesting thing, though. Sometimes it's wiser to show yourself than it is to try to sneak through a situation. You stand right out in the open like a man who has honest business. You'd be surprised how little attention people will pay to a man who doesn't act like he's doing anything wrong. They expect fugitives to hide and sneak and act suspicious. You just stroll past them right out in the open and they'll likely assume you're not the one they're looking for."

As they rode on, Dev thought about that.

Likely it was true. And then his thoughts went back to Dolph Bannerman. He said, "Noah, I've got to get hold of those papers Bannerman said he had. He knows I'm after him, so whatever I do, I've got to do it soon."

"Got a plan?"

"Not exactly. But I've been thinking about it. Bannerman said the papers were in some safe place where they'd come to light if anything were to happen to him. That means they're not buried or hid in a hollow stump or anything like that. And he's not the kind who'd leave them with someone else to hold. I figure he's got them with him. How else could he have laid hands on that newspaper clipping so quickly?"

"Where?"

"I think in his office there in the *Palace*. Probably in that big iron safe."

"Wouldn't he be afraid of it being robbed?" Noah suggested.

"The papers would be as safe there as the money he keeps in it," Dev answered. "And it's guarded. He's got Stark, Jarrett and the Breed. Likely, he keeps at least one of them in the place all the time. He probably figures it's pretty well protected."

"It probably is. . . ."

"Hard part would be getting into the office. And out again. If I could get in, I'm sure I could open that box." Dev said thoughtfully.

"You're a locksmith, too?" Noah asked.

"Back in New York I learned a bit about the craft. Never worked at it professionally, though. The fellow who was teaching me the trade got caught before I finished the course. That safe of Bannerman's is an old one and it's a pretty simple, common mechanism. I'm sure I'm good enough to get it open."

"How do you plan on getting into the office? And out again alive?"

"When I figure that out, I'll let you know."

They rode on in silence for a while and then Noah spoke. "A diversionary tactic."

"Huh?"

"Suppose something were to happen in Laramie that got the whole town's attention. Everybody, including Bannerman," he suggested. "Say a fire. I've seen what happens in these crate towns when there's a fire. It scares folks bad. If one spreads, it runs through the town in no time at all, so when there's a scare, everybody turns out to fight it. And I do mean everybody. Now, if there was a fire scare in Laramie and the folks all ran to fight it, a man with a purpose might be able to walk right into the *Palace*

191

and help himself to that safe. . . ."

"It might work," Dev muttered. "Hell, it *will* work!"

"You know the town better than I do," Noah said. "Where do you think we should start the fire?"

"I'd say maybe . . . hold on . . . I'm not asking you to get mixed up in this business with me."

"It's been a long time since I conducted on the Railway. I can't say it was ever fun, but sometimes I miss the excitement. You wouldn't deny an old man one last chance to raise a little hell, would you?"

Dev laughed. He felt a wild sense of exhilaration. Laying heels to the horse, he shouted, "Come on!"

XIV

When the two of them reached the outskirts of Laramie, they split up. Noah rode on, toward the freight station. They'd decided that in all fairness, whatever building they fired should be one of Bannerman's properties. The freight station would be easy to fire and was far enough from the surrounding buildings for the fire to be controlled if the townsfolk acted quickly. And Bannerman was sure to concern himself if it was his property on fire.

Dev dismounted on the side street that led past the *Palace.* He looped the reins of his horse over a rail of Bannerman's corral and waited there, listening for the alarm, the cry of *"fire!"*

He waited, telling himself that he'd only been there for a few moments. It seemed longer. He fingered the butt of the Colt thrust into his waistband. He pushed the hair back off his forehead. He waited.

Suddenly he started, pressing his shoulders back against the wall of the building. He tried to lose himself in the shadows. Someone was coming.

Someone had stepped through the side door and headed toward the backyard. Dev grinned humorlessly as he recognized the blanket-wrapped form and the Kossuth hat silhouetted against the lamps on the main street. From the halting way he walked, the Breed was at least half drunk.

Softly, Dev called out.

The Breed looked up, gazing puzzled into the shadows.

Dev stepped forward. Coldly, he said, "We got some unfinished business."

The Breed stood as if he were frozen, his shoulders stiff, his head thrust forward.

"Your medicine's bad," Dev was saying.

"Your luck's run out this time."

The Breed moved suddenly. Letting the blanket fall from his shoulders, he lunged toward Dev. The knife in his hand gleamed dimly in the faint light.

Dev spun on one foot, his hand wrapping around the butt of the Colt in his waistband. He felt the blade of the knife jerk into the bandage on his chest, snag in the adhesive plaster. His hand, with the gun in it, was raised. He brought it down against the back of the Breed's neck — hard. He could feel the crack of bone under the blow.

The Breed fell, face down into the mud. He lay motionless, his head cocked at a brutally awkward angle. Standing over him, Dev pointed the Navy Colt at the bare back. For a long moment he stood. Then he eased the hammer down and shoved the gun back into his waistband. He didn't need it. The Breed was dead.

He picked up the knife that had slipped from the Breed's fingers. It was a good weapon, balanced for throwing. He slipped it into his boot top. Then he wrapped the blanket around his shoulders. It covered the bandaged arm completely. With the hat pulled low over his face, he started toward the door of Bannerman's *Grand Palace* — like a man who had business to attend to and knew where he was going.

The saloon was as crowded as usual and no one seemed to pay any attention to him as he shouldered his way toward the stairs. And then he saw Jarrett.

The gunman sat on the end of his spine with his chair cocked back against the wall. His legs crossed, he rested his boots on the table in front of him. And the table was at the foot of the stairway. Dev couldn't get to those stairs without pushing past him. And Jarrett would surely notice that it wasn't the Breed under that black hat.

His head low and the blanket clutched tight around his shoulders, Dev circled back through the crowd until he was near the door. He paused there, pressing his back against the wall, ready to bolt if he had to.

How long had he been waiting? — minutes? It seemed like hours! He could feel the fear in his body, the tension in his back and arms. There was a dull ache in the injured arm that seemed to get worse when he thought about it. What had become of Noah!

Hell broke loose suddenly. There was a wild clanging of a fire iron, alarm shots, shouting from the street, and now shouting in the saloon. The music stopped short as men raced for the doors, pushing hurriedly past him and through the batwings.

He waited until they were all past, and the few people who lingered were leaning through the doors to see the excitement. Then he walked hurriedly across the floor, striding like a man who had honest business where he was going, and climbed the stairs.

The door to Bannerman's office was open, lamplight spilling into the hallway. He paused and edged up to it, listening. There was no sound. The room was empty. A twist of smoke rose from the ash tray on the desk. Evidently Bannerman had left in a hurry — at the alarm, he supposed.

He stepped in and closed the door softly behind him.

The safe was a big, old standard model that worked with a key. Dev fished a bit of bent metal out of his pocket and thrust it into the keyhole. He leaned his head against the door, listening as he worked with it. It had been a long time — his ear, his hand remembered slowly. But they did remember. And finally he heard the click. Grabbing the handle, he turned it and leaned back, hauling against the weight of the door. It swung open.

There was a small strongbox. He dragged it out, guessing from the weight that it held hard money. He pulled out account books and papers, spreading them on the floor, fingering through them, not sure how to recognize what he was looking for. Then he saw the thick, brown envelope tied with ribbon and sealed with wax. He pulled it out and read the scrawl across the front of it. Bannerman's will!

That made sense, he thought. If Bannerman were to die, it would be opened. Until then there would be no reason for anyone to disturb it. But from the look of the seal it had been opened and closed at least once. Recently, too. Probably to get out the newspaper clipping that had been circulated at End-of-Track.

He ripped off the ribbon with his teeth and tore open the envelope. Dumping its contents on the floor, he sorted through them. Another newspaper clipping, pages torn from account books, unsigned notes in an ornate handwriting. And a sheet covered with the scrawl of a telegraphist.

He scanned it rapidly. Bannerman had mentioned writing out the whole story. This was it. He gave a full account of the land-grabbing operations he and Danforth had handled for Hendon, payments taken for land purchases and charged against the company but never paid to the land owners

— and even a list of some of the properties involved. The name *Engels* caught his eye. So that was why the old man had hated Dolph Bannerman. Engrossed, he almost didn't notice the sound.

Footsteps in the hall — he froze, his hand on the Colt. They were the quick short steps of a woman. And then he heard the turning of the doorknob.

"Dolph?" she called as she pushed open the door. It was Ruby Bannerman. As she caught sight of Dev, she started. "Oh, Breed, I thought Dolph was . . . Devereaux!"

He rose to his feet as she paused, staring at him. He started toward her, and suddenly she flung herself toward him, sliding her hands over his shoulders.

"Thank God you're alive! When I sent the Breed . . . I was so afraid . . . I thought. . . ." Her hands moved on his shoulders, on the back of his neck, as she pressed her mouth to his.

He pulled away from her kiss, but she clung to him.

"Good God, Ruby! Not the Breed too!" Dolph Bannerman's voice was anguished. He stood slump-shouldered in the doorway, his collar open and his face smoke-stained. There was an old weariness in his eyes as he looked at his wife. And then he saw

Devereaux's face.

"You!" With a twist of his arm, Bannerman had the derringer in his hand. He snapped, "Ruby, get out of the way."

Her arms fell from Dev's shoulders and she stepped aside, looking questioningly at the gun in her husband's hand. "Dolph, I don't understand . . ."

Dev's fingers were on the butt of the Colt hidden by the blanket. Watching Bannerman's face, he tried to ease it out of his waistband.

"He's from Willis Siding," Bannerman told his wife. "He's come here to kill me. Haven't you, Devereaux?"

The muzzle of the Colt had cleared the waistband. Dev thrust the gun from under the blanket, thumbing back the hammer.

"Dolph!" Ruby screamed as she lunged.

The hammer fell, the gun bucking in Dev's hand as she slammed into his arm. The wall mirror shattered as the wild slug smashed into it. There was a second shot, the sharp bark of Bannerman's sleeve gun.

Ruby leaned against Dev's chest. She turned her face toward him. Her moist, coral lips parted slightly. "You filthy, lying, goddamned bastard," she said softly. Her deep green eyes clouded and she crumpled slowly to the floor.

The slug from the sleeve gun had made a small round hole between her shoulder-blades.

Bannerman stood staring at her, uncom-prehending, for a long moment. "God, oh God," he mumbled as he dropped to his knees at her side. The tiny gun slipped from his hand. He didn't seem to notice. Reach-ing out, he touched his wife's wrist.

"Ruby!" He shouted it as if he could call her back from the dead. Gently he lifted her head, the auburn curls tumbling over his hands. Over and over again he repeated her name.

Dev turned away, dragging breath into his lungs. He shoved the Colt back into his waistband and scooped up the papers he'd spilled. Jamming them into his pocket, he ran toward the stairs. At the top step, he jerked to a halt.

There were men in the saloon below, and more — smoke-grimed and grinning — pushing through the batwings, crowding toward the bar. *Too damned late,* he thought desperately. They'd gotten the fire out and were coming back already.

But the only way out of the building was through the saloon. And he had to get out quickly — before Bannerman recovered from his initial shock. Gathering the blanket, settling it securely on his shoulders, he started down the stairs. His hand was clutched tight on the butt of the Navy Colt under the blanket.

Head low, the hatbrim shadowing his face, he edged through the mill of men. He heard snatches of their words. And then he heard someone call out: "Hey, Breed, hold up a minute."

He started, realizing that he was the one being called. The voice was Hal Jarrett's. And it was close.

He risked looking up just as Jarrett stepped in front of him, blocking his way. Their eyes met.

"What the hell?" Jarrett grunted as Dev rammed the barrel of the Navy Colt into his stomach.

"Quiet. Don't try anything or I'll blow your guts out." Dev's voice was thin and hard-edged.

Jarrett looked at him curiously. There was no fear in his boyish face. "What the hell kinda game are you playing now?" he asked.

"This is no game," Dev said tautly. "If I have to, I'll kill you! Just turn around and walk through that door ahead of me, real easy now."

Looking a little confused, Jarrett turned slowly. And jumped. Twisting his body, he

201

side-stepped the barrel of the gun and rammed against Dev's injured arm.

As Dev staggered back, wincing with pain, he felt Jarrett's hands locking over his. The fingers dug into his wrist and wrenched at the gun. The move had been quick, so damned quick that he barely realized what had happened. And if anyone else had noticed, no one had paid any attention.

"I've had a bellyful of your goddamn games," Jarrett was saying, keeping his voice low. "You want to let go of my gun before I start a ruckus and somebody gets hurt?"

Dev eased his grip on the Colt, letting Jarrett yank it out of his hand.

Jarrett slipped his forefinger through the guard, touched his thumb to the hammer, settled the gun comfortably into his hand. He smiled at the feel of it there. As he leveled it at Dev, he asked, "What were you doing upstairs in that outfit? Where's the Breed?"

"Dead."

"Well, I won't miss him none. Let's you and me go on up to my room where we can talk quiet." He brushed the muzzle of the gun lightly against Dev's stomach. "Like you said, just turn around and walk ahead of me, real easy now."

Headhung, Dev started for the stairs.

He'd gambled and he'd lost — Jarrett was Bannerman's man and in a few minutes, Bannerman would come out of the office. . . .

Jarrett was talking. "I don't know what the hell you think . . ." His words were cut short by the muffled crack of a gunshot. He hesitated on the landing, looking up the stairs, frowning in puzzlement. And then he ran, urging Dev on with the Colt.

The smell of burnt powder was heavy in the hallway. It was spilling out of the open office door. With a jab of the gun, Jarrett shoved Dev toward it.

Dolph Bannerman lay on the floor by his wife, his cheek resting on her breast. The skin around the small hole in his temple was powder-scorched. Wisps of smoke still curled from the sleeve gun that lay under his limp fingers.

"Ruby?" Jarrett said. He sounded vaguely bewildered. "Ruby?" He dropped to his knees and touched a hand gently to her cold face. His fingertips moved across her cheek, brushed a loose curl back from her forehead.

"She's dead," he muttered, looking up at Dev as if he didn't really believe it. Then he looked at Bannerman. He lifted the limp hand away from the derringer and folded it over Bannerman's chest. Spreading his thumb and forefinger, he gently closed the unseeing eyes.

Dev stood uncertain, feeling some of Jarrett's shock, telling himself that he should grab this moment to run, but yet not quite able to make himself move.

Jarrett looked up and asked quietly, "What happened?"

Tersely, Dev told him. He ended it, saying, "I swear it was an accident, Ruby getting killed. She was trying to stop me, and his bullet caught her instead of me."

Jarrett nodded. Hoarse-voiced, subdued, he said, "She was a real handsome woman."

"Look, Hal, I . . ."

"Don't talk no more," he mumbled. He was looking at Ruby again. "It was gonna happen someday. This or something like it. But you come here and you brought it on. You made it happen. You got what you wanted. Now get." He didn't look up.

Dev started toward the door. And stopped short as he saw the man in the hallway. It was Johnny Stark. As he strode toward the office, Dev stepped back into the room. Automatically his hand went to his waistband. But Jarrett had the gun now.

"Hey, Hal, what's going on? I thought I heard . . ." Stark halted inside the doorway.

Startled, he looked down at the bodies. "I'll be damned," he muttered in curious surprise. Then he asked Jarrett, "Both dead?"

Hal nodded.

"How?"

"He shot her and then himself."

A corner of Stark's mouth twisted. His grin was ugly and self-satisfied. "I guess he finally got a gutfull of her she-bitch ways," he mumbled. Cocking his head, he looked at the bodies and then at the open door of the safe. For a moment his face was thoughtful. Then he turned his attention to Jarrett.

"Y'know, Hal, with both of them dead, there ain't nobody left to run this place, unless . . . unless somebody just takes over."

Jarrett didn't move. It was as if he didn't hear.

The grin broadened as Stark added, "I hope *you* haven't got any notions in that direction."

Hal looked up then. "Me?" he said blankly.

"No, you wouldn't, would you?" Stark muttered, obviously satisfied. "All you want is somebody to do the thinking for you and keep your bills paid. I s'pose you're worth the price. You understand? You take your orders from me now."

Jarrett was still looking at him, but he

made no reply.

Turning toward Dev, Stark started, "Breed, I think that you'd . . ." For the first time, he saw the face under the brim of the Kossuth hat. Still grinning, he jerked his hand toward the gun on his thigh. "Well, Devereaux . . ."

Dev moved. He threw himself down against the side of the desk as the gun bucked in Stark's hand. He could feel the bullet sear past his face as he went down. At the same instant, his hand wrapped around the hilt of the knife in his boot top, yanking it out.

It hit Stark as he triggered the second shot. He winced, more startled than hurt by the blade that struck his ribs and glanced off.

Dev felt pain lash through his body. He was hit. No — it was the broken arm. He'd wrenched his shoulder, tearing part of the bandaging loose as he moved. Stark's shot had gone wild, slamming into the desk and spraying splinters.

"Hold on, Johnny," he heard Jarrett snap. He saw him, still on his knees beside the body of Ruby Bannerman. The Navy Colt in his hand was turned toward Stark and the hammer under his thumb was at full-cock.

Stark's head jerked. Startled, completely puzzled, he looked into the barrel of the Colt. He raised his hands slightly, asking, "You loco, Hal? *You* can't handle an operation like this by yourself. You know damned well you can't. I'll take care of you, Hal. I'll see to it you get your fair share."

Jarrett looked almost as if he'd been slapped in the face. He made a slight gesture with the Colt toward Dev, and asked, "Ain't you got no pride, Johnny?"

"Huh?" Stark grunted.

"You put that six-gun down on the floor, real easy," Jarrett ordered.

Bewildered, Stark shook his head slowly. He looked into Jarrett's face, and at the sight of it, he bent and set the gun gently on the floor. When he had straightened up, his hands were well in the air.

"Dev," Jarrett said, keeping his eyes steady on Stark. He eased down the hammer of the Navy Colt.

Dev was on his knees, by the desk, watching uncertainly.

"All right Dev," Jarrett said. With a sudden twist of his hand, he sent the Colt sliding across the floor.

Sprawling on his face, his arm outstretched, Dev grabbed for it as Stark lunged for his own gun. His fingers closed on the butt. He jerked it up, rolling as he thumbed back the hammer and let it fall.

The gun kicked hard, throwing smoke in his face, bringing tears that blurred his vision. As he rolled, he felt the pain tear through his injured arm again. Dimly, he saw the flame of Stark's gun. He wasn't aware of hauling back the hammer again but he felt the Colt jump in his hand.

He saw Stark bulking over him, bending slightly, then falling. He saw him as a blurred heap, motionless on the floor.

He was lying on the floor himself, with the pain throbbing through his shoulder and a sudden weariness washing over him. He let his face rest against the hard planks. He was tired. Godawful tired.

"Devereaux?" he heard Jarrett ask tentatively.

He forced himself to move. He lifted his head. Slowly lifting himself on his elbow, he looked up.

"Stark's dead," Jarrett said. "Damn well time somebody hauled him down. No pride. No honor."

Squinting, Dev tried to focus on the gunman's body. His eyes still stung from the gunsmoke.

"Give me back my gun," Jarrett said. He felt the hand wrap around the Colt. Loosen-

208

ing his grip, he felt it pulled from his fingers. He saw Jarrett cradle it in both hands, and heard him ask, "You sure you're all right?"

He nodded. With effort, he braced himself, trying to get his legs under him.

"That's good," Jarrett mumbled. He held out a hand, helping Dev up. Sheepishly he added, "You're a damn fool, but I kinda promised that redheaded girl I'd fetch you back to her — alive."

On his feet now, clinging to Jarrett for support, Dev asked, "She made you promise that?"

"Yeah."

The pain in his shoulder had begun to ease and his vision was clearing. He saw that Jarrett was grinning and he grinned back. He let go his grip on Hal's arm and brushed at the lank hair on his forehead with the back of his hand. He could feel his strength coming back.

As he started for the door, he glanced over his shoulder at Jarrett and said, "You coming? I'm gonna need somebody to stand as best man at the wedding."

ABOUT THE AUTHOR

Lee Hoffman was born in Chicago, Illinois, and attended Armstrong Junior College in Savannah from 1949 to 1951. During her first college year she discovered science-fiction fandom and the vast network of correspondence and amateur publishing that it supported. She made many friends in this new world and even founded her own monthly magazine, *Quandry,* which attracted an enthusiastic audience. In addition to her interest in science-fiction, she continued to be an avid Western fan. Finally, in 1965, she completed a book-length Western of her own, *Gunfight at Laramie* (1966). Shortly after this first Western novel was accepted, Hoffman was commissioned by Ace to write a comic Western. It became her second book, *The Legend of Blackjack Sam* (1966), a novel all about "the Notorious Showdown at the O'Shea Corral." The years of writing for the amateur press and her own amusement were now paying off. *The Valdez Horses* (1967) is perhaps her masterpiece. Its emotional impact, aided by a surprise twist in the last line, make this novel difficult to forget. It received the Golden Spur Award from the Western Writers of America. In other novels such as *The Yarborough Brand* (1968) and *West of Cheyenne* (1969), no less than in *The Valdez Horses,* character and motivation are as important as details of the plot. It isn't that Hoffman skimped on action — there are fistfights, gun battles, and chases, but they serve the story rather than being the story's reason for existence. Hoffman refused to be predictable. In common with B. M. Bower before her and P. A. Bechko after, Hoffman tried her hand more than once at comic Westerns, notably in *Wiley's Move* (1973) and *The Truth About The Cannonball Kid* (1975). R. E. Briney in the second edition of the *Encyclopedia of Frontier and Western Fiction* concludes that Hoffman has always had "an enviable command of the writer's craft and the storyteller's art."

We hope you have enjoyed this Large Print book. Other Thorndike, Wheeler, Kennebec, and Chivers Press Large Print books are available at your library or directly from the publishers.

For information about current and upcoming titles, please call or write, without obligation, to:

Publisher
Thorndike Press
295 Kennedy Memorial Drive
Waterville, ME 04901
Tel. (800) 223-1244

or visit our Web site at:

http://gale.cengage.com/thorndike

OR

Chivers Large Print
published by AudioGO Ltd
St James House, The Square
Lower Bristol Road
Bath BA2 3SB
England
Tel. +44(0) 800 136919
www.audiogo.co.uk

All our Large Print titles are designed for easy reading, and all our books are made to last.